"I KNEW YOU WEREN'T DEAD..."

She hugged him still closer. "But you would have been if I hadn't done this. Do you mind?"

"No," Longarm managed. "I don't mind. Who...are you? How long have I—"

"Shh. Don't fret. My name is Annie. You're in my cabin. I found you in the mountains. By the time I got you here, you were very cold and very still."

Longarm managed a grin. "I'm warming up now," he told her. "Fast..."

→→ TABOR EVANS ←←

LONGARM

AND THE CALICO KID

A JOVE BOOK

LONGARM AND THE CALICO KID

A Jove Book / published by arrangement with
the author

PRINTING HISTORY
Jove edition / April 1983

ISBN: 0-515-06255-3

Jove books are published by Jove Publications, Inc.,
200 Madison Avenue, New York, N.Y. 10016. The words
"A JOVE BOOK" and the "J" with sunburst are trademarks
belonging to Jove Publications, Inc.

PRINTED IN THE UNITED STATES OF AMERICA

LONGARM

AND THE CALICO KID

Prologue

The judge looked at the jury foreman as if he were mad.

"Would you repeat that verdict?" he demanded. Like the judge, everyone in the hushed courtroom was incredulous.

The jury foreman, a pale, skinny fellow, swallowed and said, his voice quavering, "Not guilty, Your Honor."

"Would you care to explain your verdict to this court?" the judge demanded. His face was beet red and his gray hair appeared to stand straight up, so aroused was he.

"Well, Judge," the foreman explained, shifting his feet nervously, "we just ain't heard enough evidence to hang Hardy, is all."

The spectators gasped. With an angry exclamation, a girl in the rear stood up and fled the courtroom. Wallace, the deputy U.S. marshal who had collared Wes Hardy, stood up to look more closely at the jury foreman. The judge gaveled him back into his seat.

Sitting at the table beside his lawyer, Wes Hardy leaned back in his chair, grinning. He was a big, beefy man with small, cruel eyes. His red hair was thick and unkempt, straggling over the shoulders of his dirty buckskin jacket.

The judge glowered at the jury. "It wouldn't do me any good to poll you men, I suppose," he said, his voice laced with contempt.

The members of the jury shook their heads. Some looked defiant; others had smirks on their faces. Not one of them appeared about to change his vote.

"Wes Hardy!" the judge said, turning to the defendant. "Stand up!"

Hardy stood up, his mean eyes fixing the judge's coldly. There was not an ounce of contrition in the man's manner. He had the winning hand, and he knew it.

"This here jury has seen fit to ignore the evidence and declare you not quilty of the killing of Inspector Carl Reese, which crime you did commit in cold blood and without mercy before honest witnesses. Nevertheless, by laws of this land, I have no recourse but to set you free. But do not think you have escaped justice, Wes Hardy. You will find yourself standing before another Judge when the time comes—as it must to all men—and before that court you will not escape your just and proper punishment!"

The judge brought his gavel down with a powerful crack, got up, and stalked out of the courtroom.

Chapter 1

Chief Marshal Billy Vail pulled himself together and, shaking his head, slumped into his seat behind his desk. Glancing wearily at Longarm, he growled, "I knew something like this would happen. When that crazy jury let Wes Hardy off after he killed Carl Reese, it was only a matter of time."

Lowering his tall frame into Vail's red leather armchair, Longarm took out a fresh cheroot and cocked an eye at the chief. "Did I hear you right?" Longarm asked. "You say someone who calls himself the Calico Kid's been knocking off the jurors who let Hardy off?"

Vail nodded decisively. "That's what's happening, Longarm."

"You got any idea who this Calico Kid might be?"

"Someone who sure as hell don't like what that jury done when it let Hardy off for killin' Reese, that's for sure. The son of a bitch has already picked off three jurors. Find him, Longarm. And fast. This is my district. I don't want any more damned telegrams from Washington."

Longarm lit his cheroot. Exhaling a fragrant cloud into the air above his head, he drawled, "Now, what say we eat this here apple one bite at a time, Chief. I'll get the son of a bitch, but I need some background. I just got in, remember."

Vail ran a pudgy hand over his face, brushed back his thinning hair, and proceeded to bring the tall lawman up to date. He began with Wes Hardy's killing of Carl Reese, a government inspector who was checking over the herd Hardy had brought down from the mountains. Hardy, a professional drover, had brought in some beef that were carrying more than a few questionable brands, and as soon as the inspector began looking too closely, Hardy pulled out his sixgun and cut Reese down. Hardy was held on the spot and Wallace brought him in for trial.

"And then, goddammit," Vail growled, "that crazy jury let the drover off. Not enough evidence, they said. And, since then, three of the jury members have been shot down in cold blood. The latest was Sam Tolliver in Bent Creek."

Longarm took another drag on his cheroot. He knew where Bent Creek was—about thirty miles south of Denver.

"So the Calico Kid is now in the process of cutting down everyone in that jury who let Hardy off."

"That's the way it looks to me."

"Then I'll want a list of the jurors. The dead ones along with the live ones. Maybe I can get to them in time to put a stop to this foolishness."

"Jesus, Longarm. No maybe about it. You've got to stop him before he kills any more of them."

Longarm shrugged. "I'll do what I can, Chief. But this here Calico Kid has a pretty good start on me already. He's probably stalking one of them fool jurors right this minute while we're sitting here. What can you give me for a description of the Kid?"

Vail sighed. "Not much. After Tolliver was cut down, the townsmen saw a lean kid riding hell bent for leather out of town. He was wearing a calico bandanna over his face. It was the Calico Kid, all right."

"What was he riding?"

"A bay."

Longarm got to his feet, dropped his dead cheroot into the spittoon next to Billy Vail's desk, then glanced up at the banjo clock on the wall.

"I'll go on back to my digs and pick up my gear," he told Vail. "When I return, I'll want all you can give me on Carl Reese and Wes Hardy—along with that list of jurors."

"You'll have it," Vail said, getting to his feet also.

For a moment Longarm glanced at the marshal, noting once again how much his boss had gone to lard in the time Vail had taken over his post. A man who in this salad days had tracked many a killer to his lair, Billy Vail was now reduced to tracking down memos and battling the blizzard of paperwork emanating from Washington.

"Don't worry, Billy," Longarm drawled as he started for the door. "This won't be all that tough. All I'll have to do is keep an eye on them jurors. You might say each of the damn fools has earned the right to bait my trap— since they were foolish enough to let Wes Hardy off in the first place."

5

Vail peered gloomily across the room at Longarm. "Don't forget, Longarm, the government's already lost one man."

With a reflective nod, Longarm opened the door and left.

The town of Bent Creek, just thirty miles south of Denver City on the high plains, was asleep in the sun. Its wide main street, a rutted, dusty thoroughfare, was free of traffic, and as Longarm clopped noisily over the wooden bridge that spanned the creek and rode on into the town, he noted the town drunk sprawled like a sack of soiled clothing on the bench in front of Mulligan's Palace, the town's only saloon.

As Longarm rode closer, only the lush's eyes moved in their sockets to follow his progress. The rest of his torso remained as immobile as the carcass of a dead buffalo. Guiding his horse to the hitch rail in front of the saloon, Longarm dismounted, dropped his reins over the weathered rail, and mounted the porch steps. Ignoring the drunk, he paused to look the town over.

It didn't look any better from the porch than it had from his saddle. Two men had appeared on the boardwalk across the street and were watching him carefully. Longarm let his glance fall lightly over the lush still sprawled on the bench, then pushed through the bat wings into the saloon.

The place was empty except for the barkeep, a burly fellow with a red garter on his sleeve and thinning black hair plastered like leather down over his bullet-shaped skull. He sported a meticulously oiled, pencil-thin mustache, dark hard eyes, and the jowls of a bulldog. He was polishing a beer glass and did not pause when Longarm rested his elbows on the bar and nudged his Stetson back off his forehead. It had been a long, hot ride.

"Beer," he told the barkeep.

The barkeep drew the beer. Before serving Longarm, he swept off the excess foam with the back of his hand. Longarm paid the man and lifted the beer to his lips. Sipping it, he smiled at the barkeep.

The barkeep did not smile back.

"This here the town where the Calico Kid shot Sam Tolliver?"

"Who the hell are you?" growled the barkeep. "One of them Eastern dudes come looking for an eyewitness story?"

"Golly!" cried Longarm in utter astonishment. "How in the world did you guess?"

For a moment the barkeep was fooled. Then his eyes narrowed as he looked Longarm over more closely. What the man saw was someone on the comfortable side of forty whose lean face had withstood the lash of uncounted winds and felt the branding iron of too many suns. His rawboned features were cured to a saddle-leather brown so pronounced he might have been mistaken for an Indian had it not been for the blue of his wide-set eyes, the tobacco-leaf color of his hair, and his uptwisted longhorn mustache.

"Aw, shit," said the barkeep. "You sure as hell ain't from the East. So who are you, and how come you're asking about the Calico Kid?"

Smiling, Longarm said, "I'm a deputy U.S. marshal come to look into the death of Sam Tolliver, one of your local citizens killed by the Calico Kid. Maybe you can help."

The barkeep relaxed. "I knew damn well you wasn't no New York writer." He held out his hand. Longarm shook it. "I'm Zeke Mulligan."

"So what can you tell me about Sam Tolliver's killing, Mulligan? Were you in town when he was shot?"

"Sure," Zeke said. "I heard the shot myself and saw the Calico Kid ride out."

"Where was Tolliver shot?"

"In the alley behind the saloon. Leastways, that's where we found the poor son of a bitch after we heard the shot. His pants was still unbuttoned. Not long after that, the Calico Kid went riding on out of here like there was a beehive up his ass."

Longarm frowned and sipped his beer. "This here Calico Kid likes to get his men with their britches down, that it?"

"Maybe yes, maybe no. He got Sam Tolliver that way, but not Paul Dudley. He nailed Dudley in Mule Canyon, ten miles west of here. There was no privy in sight."

"And the other one—Pete Jacobs?"

"He got old Pete when he was out mendin' his fence. His wife found him belly-up in his stock's water hole."

"How come they call him the Calico Kid?"

"He hides his face with a calico bandanna. And he's a kid, sure enough—as thin as rail."

Longarm finished his beer.

"Have another on the house," Mulligan said, drawing Longarm a fresh beer and shoving it toward him across the polished bar.

Longarm drank deep, relishing the cold beer. "Things have quieted down some in this town, I notice," he remarked. "Just had another funeral?"

"Nope. And we ain't plannin' on none, either. That's why the town is so quiet. Wes Hardy is asleep in the hotel across the street, and he likes it nice and peaceful when he sleeps. He threw one roomer out of a window for snoring too loud in the room next to his."

"It's past noon. He's still sleeping?"

"That's right. He plays all night and sleeps all day. He's a bear of a man and twice as mean."

"Was Wes Hardy in town when Tolliver was shot down?"

"Sure."

"And Wes is across the street sleeping now."

"That's what I said. Less'n all that noise you made ridin' over the bridge woke him up. You made quite a racket, you know."

"Reckon I did at that," Longarm acknowledged, downing the rest of his beer. He started from the saloon. "Thanks," he said.

"You leavin' town?"

"Not just yet. Thought I ought to mosey over and wake up the son of a bitch who started all this. Shake a tree and you don't know what might fall out."

"You must be crazy, Deputy."

Longarm didn't bother to reply as he pushed his way through the bat wings. He wasn't crazy. He just wanted to know what Wes Hardy had done to get that jury to let him off. And the best way to find that out would be to wake the lazy bastard up and ask him.

Wes Hardy swore and sat up. The knock came again, louder this time. The door reverberated violently. Hardy flung back his covers and sat up, angrily pulling on his Levi's and boots.

He was six feet four inches tall. His short-sleeved red flannel shirt hung open, revealing a chest covered with a mass of coiled, rust-colored hair. He was a man in his mid-thirties with massive shoulders and powerful arms. A red stubble covered his rawboned cheeks and, as he glanced at the door, still reverberating to the impatient knocking, his eyes held a mad light in them.

Brushing a huge hand through his mop of flaming red hair, Hardy strode to the door. Yanking it open, he cried, "What's the matter with you, Smith? I told you I ain't to be disturbed!"

But it was not the desk clerk. Hardy was confronted by a lean, tall drink of water with a slight grin on his face. "Afternoon, Mr. Hardy," the big fellow drawled. "I hope I didn't disturb you."

"You know damn well you did. Who in blazes are you?"

"Deputy U.S. Marshal Custis Long."

"A lawman?"

"That's right."

Hardy flung the door shut in Longarm's face and started back to his rumpled bed. Behind him, the door was kicked open so sharply that it slammed against the wall. Turning swiftly, Hardy strode forward and reached out with both hands. Grabbing the lawman by the lapels of his fancy frock coat, he flung him back out through the doorway.

The lawman slammed against the wall opposite his door, and Hardy began cuffing him in the face with his open hand. When the lawman flung up his arms in an effort to block his punches, Hardy just laughed and, stepping closer, pummelled the lawman unmercifully about the head and shoulders with clenched fists until the lawman sagged, barely conscious, to the floor.

Hardy's blood was up by this time. He bent and plucked the Colt from the lawman's cross-draw ring and proceeded to pistol-whip him with brutal efficiency. Then, still grinning, he straightened up, leveled the Colt and sighted along the barrel. He was aiming at the lawman's right eye, his finger tightening on the trigger, when some-

10

thing exploded in the lawman's hand.

A whore's gun! The son of a bitch had a whore's gun! Hardy felt the slug whisper past him as he pulled the Colt's trigger. His slug powdered the plaster inches above the lawman's head as the derringer jumped a second time in the lawman's hand. This time, Hardy felt the round slam into his left shouder.

He dropped the Colt as the surprising force of the .44 slug sent him reeling back into his room.

Through a red haze, Longarm lurched to his feet, picked his fallen Colt off the floor, and followed Wes Hardy back into his room. Behind him he heard the sound of feet running on the hotel stairs, but he paid it no mind as he slammed the door shut and approached the wounded Hardy.

The man was sitting up on the edge of the bed, his right hand clasped over his bleeding shoulder wound. Blood was pouring through his fingers in a steady, pulsing flow. Longarm shoved the muzzle of his double-action Colt under the man's chin, then dug it in. The big redhead leaned back, gasping, as he felt the barrel digging into his throat.

"Damn you!" he managed. "I can't breathe!"

A second before his finger tightened on the trigger, Longarm moved the barrel. The gun detonated, its thunderous roar filling the small room as the .44 slug seared past Hardy's chin and slammed into the ceiling above his head.

Then Longarm poked the barrel deep into Hardy's gut.

"I won't move it this time, you son of a bitch," muttered Longarm through his bleeding, swollen lips. "So just give me a reason to pull this trigger. You got off with that jury, but you won't get off this time."

"All right! All right!" Hardy cried, his stubbled face revealing something close to panic. "Don't shoot, for Christ's sake!"

"I want to know why that jury let you off."

"They knew I'd kill them, or have my friends do it, if they convicted me for killing Reese."

"But you couldn't count on intimidating all of them. So some you paid to make sure the other members of the jury went along." Longarm leaned closer, his eyes narrowing. "That's right, ain't it?"

Grudgingly, his eyes burning into Longarm's, Hardy nodded. "That's right. Some I paid."

"Who'd you pay?"

"I ain't tellin'!"

Longarm dug the barrel in deeper. Still clutching at his wounded shoulder, Hardy tried to draw back, but he could not escape the relentless pressure.

"Damn you!" Hardy cried. "It was Bill Rawlings of the Diamond K."

"Who else?"

Hardy seemed ready to rebel despite the gun pressing into his midsection. Smiling, Longarm dug it in still deeper.

"Howard Murphy," Hardy gasped painfully, "of the Lazy M."

"Anyone else?"

"No!"

"That's better. Now, what do you know about the Calico Kid?" Longarm asked.

"Nothing."

Longarm studied the big man for a moment, then decided to see how far he could push. So far, he had been able to shake quite a bit from this particular tree.

Pressing his Colt a bit more deeply into Hardy's gut, Longarm said, "I think you're lying, Hardy."

"I don't know nothin' about that crazy son of a bitch. He's just goin' around shootin' everybody that was on that jury. Hell, I ain't got nothin' against them folks what let me off! The hell with all these questions, damn you! I'm bleeding to death. I need a doctor!"

The door behind them opened. Longarm stepped back from the bed and turned, his .44 still covering Hardy. A harried, gray-haired woman swept into the room. Behind her came her pasty-faced desk clerk. He had an oversized Colt in his hand, which trembled dangerously as he followed the woman into the room.

Once inside the room, the gray-haired woman halted to stare with some concern at Hardy's shoulder wound. But when she turned from Hardy to look at Longarm's battered visage, she gasped, her hand flying up to her mouth.

"I'm a deputy U. S. Marshal, ma'am," Longarm told her, realizing for the first time that his left nostril was pouring blood. "And who might you be?"

"Carol Romey," the woman managed, her wide blue eyes showing concern for him. "I own this hotel."

"Well, I'd appreciate it if you'd tell your friend over there to put down that Colt and go fetch a doctor. Unless you'd rather have Hardy bleed to death right here."

With a frantic, pleading look, she turned to the desk clerk. "Kenny, please—will you go?"

With a quick, relieved nod, the clerk stuck the cannon into his belt and disappeared out the door.

Longarm smiled painfully at the woman. "I can understand how Kenny feels, but I was afraid that big Colt of his might go off."

"I don't think it was loaded," she said hastily. "My,

13

your face looks terrible. I think you should have it looked at."

"I don't usually look this bad," he admitted, "but I got off on the wrong foot with Wes Hardy, here."

Hardy groaned and sagged back onto the bed, still clutching at his torn shoulder.

Longarm glanced down at him. "Don't worry, Hardy, you won't die. I won't let you. I'm taking you in for jury tampering. If we can't get you for the killing of that inspector, we'll get you for whatever we can."

"You son of a bitch. I'll deny everything."

"Maybe you will. But I don't think Rawlings will— or Murphy."

Without warning, Hardy's bloody right hand lashed out, knocking the gun from Longarm's grasp. Leaping to his feet, the wounded man barged past Longarm and bolted out the door. Longarm relaxed and sat back down on the bed as he heard the ruckus Hardy made charging down the stairs. He picked up his Colt and walked over to the window to watch as Hardy flung himself onto his horse and galloped out of town.

He turned to the gray-haired woman and holstered his gun. "Looks like Hardy wasn't hurt as bad as it seemed."

"That don't matter," she said. "I'm glad to get that animal out of my hotel. For that I thank you, Deputy."

Kenny came back into the room as Carol Romey spoke. There was no doctor in his wake, but he wore a broad grin. "He's gone, Mrs. Romey," the clerk cried happily. "I just saw him ride out. Wes Hardy's gone!"

"You can thank this gentleman for that," she told him.

Kenny turned to Longarm, his eyes wide. "Thanks a lot, mister! You don't know what it was like with that man rooming here. We were losing boarders right and left."

14

Longarm smiled at the clerk and waved away the thanks, then finished reloading his derringer, clipped it back onto his watch chain, and dropped it into his right vest pocket. Nodding goodbye to the two of them, he left the room.

As he descended the stairs, he gently massaged his swollen jaw and checked his nose. Satisfied that it was no longer bleeding, he reflected with grim satisfaction that he had accomplished what he had intended. Wes Hardy now had a damn good reason for going after Rawlings or Murphy and either shutting them up or warning them. And, whichever he did, Longarm would have him.

It was true he had been sent out here primarily to bring in the Calico Kid, but it was also true that until the Calico Kid surfaced again, Billy Vail would not be at all unhappy if Longarm managed to bring in Hardy.

Wes Hardy might have escaped one jury, but justice would get another chance.

Chapter 2

Bill Rawlings hurried from the barn, took one look at the incoming rider, and groaned. Joanna had run from the cabin to tell him of Wes Hardy's approach.

"Something's wrong with him," she told her husband. "He's riding without a hat."

She was a tall, angular woman with prematurely gray hair piled into an untidy bun on the top of her head. The two of them made a fine match. Bill had as lean and wiry a figure as Joanna's, but there the token resemblance ended, for his eyes were as dark as an Indian's, with hair to match. The childless couple had owned the Diamond K for eighteen hardscrabble years.

"He's been wounded, looks like," Bill muttered, starting across the yard to meet Hardy.

Before Bill could reach him, Wes had pulled up and then slipped slowly off his horse. Grabbing hold of his saddlehorn to steady himself, he glared through pain-filled eyes at Bill as the rancher halted before him.

"Get me inside, Bill," he demanded. "I been shot."

"How bad are you hurt?"

"Never mind that. Get me inside."

Bill swallowed. "Sure, Wes. Sure thing. Here, let me give you a hand."

Moving in closer, Bill let Wes drape his arm over his shoulders, then helped him across the yard into their cabin. Joanna was waiting inside. She closed the door after them, followed them into the bedroom, and watched as Bill let Wes down on their own bed. His huge bulk almost sank out of sight in the soft, yielding embrace of their spacious feather bed.

Then Bill stepped back and let his wife look at the wounded man.

"It's just a flesh wound," said Joanna, as she examined Wes's shoulder closely. "The bullet's gone clean through. I'll dress it. Once we stop the bleeding, Wes should be all right."

Wes had been lying with his eyes closed. He opened them and looked up at her. "Get right to it, Joanna. There's a deputy U. S. marshal on my tail."

She nodded grimly and hurried from the room.

Looking down at Wes, Bill asked, "He the one shot you?"

Hardy nodded. "He's a big son of a bitch. And tricky. Shot me with a whore's gun. I told him, Bill—about me payin' you and Howie to turn that jury."

"That wasn't such a good idea, was it, Wes? It was Howie gave you the money in the first place."

Wes grinned meanly. "Maybe it wasn't exactly the

18

truth, at that. But now he'll be after you and Howie, not just me."

"Damn you, Wes. Why couldn't you keep your mouth shut? Now we got this deputy to worry about, along with the Calico Kid."

"Yup. That's the way it looks, all right. Now we're all in this together."

Bill did not like it. The thousand dollars Wes had given him to intimidate that jury had enabled Bill to pay off his remaining mortgage and buy new breeding stock. He was set now—or so he had thought until the Calico Kid began his killings.

Joanna returned and began to cut away Wes's red flannel shirt to get to the wound.

"I'll take care of his horse," Bill said.

He turned and left the room. He had some thinking to do.

Bill had returned to the cabin and was on his second cup of coffee when Joanna entered the kitchen. Without a word to him she went over to the sink, poured some water into a kettle, and placed it on the stove. Then she fed the stove fresh firewood and turned to her husband letting out a deep sigh.

"What's that for?" he asked.

"I want to wash my hands thoroughly," she said, holding out her bloody palms so he could see them.

He looked away. "How is he?"

"I've stopped the bleeding. He's asleep now." She walked over and sat down carefully, preventing her hands from touching anything. "Bill, what are we going to do?"

"I been thinking on that. How long do you think it'll take for him to be able to ride out of here?"

"He lost a little blood, that's all. He'll be up and

around as soon as he gets his strength back. That shouldn't be more than a few days."

"Too bad," Bill said.

"What do you mean?"

"You know what I mean."

"No, I don't."

Frowning, she looked at him for a while, considering. Bill watched her. She knew what he meant, all right.

The heat from the stove filled the kitchen as the water in the kettle began to boil. Joanna left the table, poured the water into a dishpan on the counter beside the sink, and mixed it with fresh spring water from the pump. Using a large bar of yellow soap, she scrubbed her hands and forearms with a vicious intensity, pouring the rest of the heated water into the pan as needed. At last, when she had completely scrubbed off Wes Hardy's blood she dried herself with a towel and sat back down at the table.

"All right, I know what you're thinking," she said. "But I don't like it."

"I don't like it, either. But can you think of a better way to get rid of him? We got enough trouble with the Calico Kid. We don't need any more from the law."

"He came to us for help. He's a wounded man."

"He's a killer, and you know it. He would as soon kill us as look at us if it served his purpose."

"So you suggest that we kill him to serve our own."

"He that lives by the sword shall die by the sword."

"I don't like Wes Hardy. And I don't like what you did when you let him bribe you. But it's done and there's no way we can undo it. Still, killing Wes Hardy would be murder."

"You forget. His testimony could put me in jail. He has already told this deputy that he bribed me and Howie to hang that jury. But if he was dead, he could no longer

20

testify against us. And his mouth would be shut good and proper."

She got up from the table, brought back a pot of coffee and two cups and saucers, and filled both cups. As was her custom, she drank hers black. "You say he *was* guilty of killing that inspector?"

Sensing that he was winning her over, he nodded. "As guilty as sin. Inspector Reese was an old fool, but we all liked him. He looked the other way more than once when me and Howie brought in mavericks from time to time. You remember. Reese was not a bad sort."

"No," she admitted, "he wasn't."

"Do you want Wes Hardy under our roof for the next couple of weeks, Joanna?" he asked softly. "You remember that last time—"

"You don't have to remind me," she snapped, putting down her empty cup. "He's an animal."

Bill straightened. The harsh, grating tone of her voice and the sudden cold light in her eyes told him that she would go along. His lips were dry and he felt slightly dizzy. They were comtemplating murder, pure and simple: and here they were drinking coffee together and discussing it as calmly as if they were considering the purchase of a horse.

"Will you do it?" Joanna asked.

Bill nodded, his mouth now as dry as sawdust. "Go see if he's still asleep."

Joanna hesitated for only a moment. Then she got up from the table and walked into the bedroom.

The Calico Kid had seen Wes Hardy arrive at the Diamond K and was pleased. She would get both of them—Rawlings and Hardy. For just a moment as she watched Bill Rawlings help Hardy into the cabin, she had contemplated riding up at that moment and cutting them both down.

But she knew Joanna and did not want to kill her, and it was unlikely that she would be able to kill the two men without having to cut down Joanna at the same time. So she had decided to wait.

As the three disappeared into the cabin, she pulled her bay back into the draw, dismounted, and tied it up to a cottonwood sapling. Then, her Colt clutched in her small right hand, she started toward the Rawlings's cabin, moving in a long, circuitous route.

She was a slight figure in her blue cotton shirt and Levi's, the bottoms of which she wore tucked into her riding boots. She had taken the precaution of binding her small breasts securely under her shirt. Her calico bandanna hung loosely about her neck. She wore a floppy-brimmed black hat, the crown of which was high enough to contain the massive pile of straw-colored hair she kept hidden under it. Looking out from under its broad brim was a surprisingly boyish face with ice-cold blue eyes.

With her breasts bound, she resembled a young boy of nineteen or so as she scrambled over the gently rolling prairie, guided by the squeak of Rawlings's windmill. When, after a moment or two, she got within sight of it, she kept her eye on it, but still continued to approach the house from an angle, keeping low to the ground.

Coming up on the cabin from the rear, she deftly skirted a ramshackle hen house and a foul-smelling pig-pen. At her approach, a Rhode Island red opened its wings and flew off, cackling unhappily. Watching it disappear around the corner of the cabin, the Calico Kid flattened herself against the log side of the cabin and lifted the bandanna to cover her face. Carefully, she inched her way along until she was able to peer through

22

the bedroom window. What she saw astounded her.

Bill Rawlings stood beside the sleeping Hardy and peered down at the man he was about to murder. The Smith and Wesson hung heavily in his right hand. He swallowed— or tried to—and raised the gun until he was sighting down its barrel at Wes's right eye.

The eye opened.

The gun in Rawlings's hand began to shake uncontrollably. Behind him, Bill heard Joanna swear. She strode into the room and snatched the weapon from his trembling grasp to do the job herself.

But she was not fast enough. With an oath that shook the room, Wes Hardy leaped from the bed and, with one powerful swipe of his massive arm, knocked Joanna violently to one side. She struck the wall with a sickening crunch as the weapon in her hand thumped to the floor. In an instant, Hardy had snatched up the gun and turned on Bill, his face contorted with fury.

"No, Wes!" Rawlings cried, backing hastily away. "Jesus, Wes! Have mercy!"

"Sure!" barked Wes. "Why not?"

He aimed the weapon at Rawlings's gut and fired. As Rawlings staggered back against the bureau drawer, clutching as his vitals, Hardy fired a second time, an inch or two lower. With a high, terrified scream of agony, Rawlings slumped to the floor and began to writhe in his own bloody gore.

With a bone-chilling cry of rage, Joanna flung herself on Hardy. The force of her charge sent him momentarily back against the wall. But he recovered from her attack enough to stay on his feet and strike out at her with the barrel of the Smith and Wesson. The blows caught her with terrible effect about the face and head until she slumped, senseless, to the floor.

Hardy took her by the hair and dragged her from the room. He pulled the door shut after him so as not to be bothered by the moans of her dying husband and then pulled her brutally up onto the long horsehair sofa that sat against one wall of the cabin's living room.

She was only barely conscious when he raped her.

Staggered by the brutality of what she had just witnessed, the Calico Kid turned her head away from the window and stepped back.

She had come to the Diamond K to kill Bill Rawlings, as she had vowed to do on old Carl Reese's grave. And now she told herself she must be pleased to see him get his just reward for letting Hardy escape the hangman. But it was Hardy she really wanted—more than ever now.

She glanced back into the room in time to see Hardy drag Joanna from it. It was obvious what the aroused Wes Hardy was now about to do to her.

Holstering her weapon, the Calico Kid turned and ran swiftly back to the draw where she had left her bay. When she reached the draw, she found that her mount had pulled loose from the sapling. For a moment she thought it was gone, until she caught sight of it cropping grass behind a boulder. Reaching the bay, she leaped into the saddle, then dug her heels into its sides.

Galloping up to the cabin, she hauled her horse to a sliding stop and punched a shot into the sky.

"Wes Hardy!" she cried.

There was no response from the cabin. Again she fired into the heavens.

This time the cabin door opened a crack. Bending low over her mount, she charged the door, firing at it as she

24

came. She saw the heavy slugs bite into the flimsy wood. The door flew open. Hardy slumped, wounded, in the doorway—and in the cabin behind Hardy, the woman he had just beaten unmercifully was rushing toward the open doorway, a revolver in her hand.

Certain that Joanna would do all she could to help her, the Calico Kid dismounted, uncoiled her rope, and strode swiftly toward Wes Hardy. He had pitched slightly forward in the doorway now, his head hanging out over the sill. The Calico Kid smiled. She was about to give Wes Hardy the just hanging he had escaped.

But, to the Kid's amazement, Joanna flung up the revolver Hardy had dropped and began to blaze away at her from the open doorway. She was in such a fury that her aim was faulty, but that did not mean she was not dangerous.

Flinging herself to one side, the Calico Kid unholstered her own weapon and returned Joanna's fire. She was unable to get a clear shot, however, as the woman dragged the unconscious Wes Hardy into the cabin and slammed the door shut.

The Calico Kid sprang to her feet, amazed and completely befuddled. That woman was crazy. Wes Hardy had just gutshot her husband, and she was saving his life.

The Calico Kid shook her head. If she lived to be a hundred, she would never be able to understand some women.

She darted back to her horse and swung into the saddle. As she did so, a shot came from one of the windows. The round whispered over her right shoulder as she wheeled her bay and galloped away from the cabin.

It was not until she had reached the low hills surrounding the Diamond K that she saw the horseman trailing her. With an exasperated groan, she turned her powerful mount toward Mule Canyon and let it have its head.

Longarm's mount was too far gone at this point to overtake the rider, so he pulled up within sight of the canyon, dismounted to give his horse a breather, then started walking back to the Diamond K, leading the horse. When he finally reached the spread, it was close to dusk.

"Hello!" he called.

A tall woman with ragged gray hair pulled open the door and looked out at him warily. As she did so, Longarm noticed the door's condition. Someone had blown holes in it with a powerful gun. The Calico Kid, more than likely.

"Who're you?" the woman demanded.

"Deputy U. S. Marshal Long, ma'am. A little while ago I heard some shots, and I saw the Calico Kid riding away from here."

She pushed the door open wider and stepped out of the doorway. Longarm took that for an invitation to enter and dismounted. The woman was nowhere in sight when he doffed his cap and strode into the living room. He saw the open bedroom door and headed for it.

He found her in the bedroom, sitting in a wooden chair beside a dead man, who was obviously her husband. The dead man seemed about to vanish entirely from sight as he lay in the center of the large feather bed. He was staring up at the ceiling with his hands crossed over his chest. A dark stain covered his lower torso. The stench of death hung in the room. Longarm's eyes caught sight of another stain on the floor in front of the bureau.

"Ma'am," he said, "who did this?"

"The Calico Kid," she replied bitterly.

Longarm put his hat back on. "Next time," he said, "I'll ride a little harder."

"You do that, Deputy," she snapped, without looking at him. "And now will you leave me be?"

Longarm nodded to the woman's bowed head, turned, and left the cabin. As he rode out of the Diamond K, something told him that all was not as it appeared. As crazy as it sounded, that dead man on the feather bed seemed to be trying to tell him something.

And besides, where was Wes Hardy? It was *his* tracks Longarm had followed to the Diamond K.

Chapter 3

It was early the next morning when Longarm reached Howard Murphy's Lazy M.

The Lazy M was considerably different from the Diamond K. The main house was a massive, gleaming white, two-story frame dwelling built in the style of a Southern mansion. It had a veranda that extended the full length of the house and an elaborate railed balcony on the veranda's roof. French windows led from the balcony into the rooms on the second floor.

The outbuildings seemed almost as solidly constructed as the main house. There was a cookshack, bunkhouse, three barns, and a blacksmith shop. All of them were planted neatly about the large compound. Each building was painted a solid gray and no ridge poles sagged. The fences were whitewashed for the most part, and well kept.

A stand of cottonwoods flanked the main building, shading many of the outbuildings as well. Behind the ranch rose the foothills of the Rockies, and in the early morning haze, the pile of mountain peaks towering over them looked much closer than they really were. Though they were fifty miles distant, to any rider who did not know better it would appear that he was but a few hours' ride from their cool foothills.

As Longarm approached the main gate, a rider with a rifle across his pommel rode out to meet him. Longarm pulled up to wait for him. Reining in his mount, the Lazy M hand seemed polite enough as he touched the brim of his hat in greeting.

"You're on Lazy M land, mister," he said laconically, his gray eyes studying Longarm coldly. "State your business or ride off."

Longarm took out his wallet containing his shield and passed it to the rider. "Name's Custis Long," he explained. "Come to see Howard Murphy."

"You mind telling me what this is all about?"

"I'd rather tell Murphy."

The man smiled and handed back Longarm's wallet. "I know that, Deputy," he said slowly, as if he were talking to a backward child. "But tell me first, why don't you? And then I'll go tell Mr. Murphy, and then he'll tell me if he wants to see you."

Longarm looked for a long moment at the fellow. "Tell him it is about the Calico Kid. And that I just came from the late Bill Rawlings's spread."

"Did you say the *late* Bill Rawlings?"

"I did. Rawlings is dead. Seems I was just a little too far behind the Kid to do Rawlings much good."

"Stay here," the rider said, wheeling his horse.

Longarm waited patiently as the rider rode back to the main house. It wasn't long before he returned for Longarm and escorted him into the Lazy M compound. Longarm saw a stocky fellow he assumed was the owner of the ranch emerge from the big house and come to a halt on the veranda.

"Here he is, Mr. Murphy," the cowboy said.

"Thanks, Mel," the big fellow said, watching Longarm closely as he rode up to the house.

Mel rode off as Longarm dismounted and dropped his reins over the hitch rail in front of the porch. As soon as Longarm had gained the veranda, Murphy strode forward to greet him.

"Come in out of the hot sun, Deputy," he said, clapping Longarm heartily on the back as he shook his hand. "It is probably too early for civilized men to drink. But no one who lives in this forsaken wilderness of wind and grass could possibly be considered civilized."

Murphy showed Longarm into the sitting room. Longarm was prompted to take off his hat as he looked about him at the bare, vast room. It was a long cavernous affair with a fireplace dominating the far wall and a huge buffalo rug covering the floor. Trophies and rifles crowded the walls. There were no paintings or ornaments, and it was immediately apparent that the Lazy M was strictly a male kingdom. Nowhere was the touch of a woman's softening hand visible.

As Longarm sat down in a leather armchair, a liveried Indian houseboy approached him to find out what he wanted to drink.

"Rye," Longarm told the boy. "Maryland, if you have it."

"Capital! I'll have the same," Murphy told the boy,

sitting down in a high, uncomfortable-looking wooden chair covered with an Indian blanket. It was obviously Murphy's favorite seat.

The owner of the Lazy M was a heavy-set fellow with a full shock of white hair that contrasted sharply with his ruddy complexion. His eyes were dark brown and sharp, his face showing little slack, despite his age, which must have been at least fifty.

As the houseboy left the room, Murphy leaned forward, a sudden frown on his face. "Now, what can you tell me about the death of Bill Rawlings?"

Longarm told the man what he had seen as he approached the Diamond K, and of his futile chase of the Calico Kid. When he described Bill's solitary wife sitting by the body of her dead husband, Murphy shook his head in sympathy.

"Those two ran the Diamond K alone, did they?" Longarm asked.

Murphy nodded solemnly. "They had no children, and lately they have been unable to afford any hired help. It has been a struggle for them. And now this . . ."

"It might be a good idea for you to send a few of your men over to help the woman out for now," Longarm suggested.

"Of course. That's an excellent idea."

"This all started because of that trial, Murphy," Longarm reminded him, "and the fact that the jury let Wes Hardy off even though he was guilty of cutting down Carl Reese. So, if you don't mind, I have a few questions I'd like to ask."

Their drinks arrived. Murphy waited until the houseboy had left before he responded. "By all means, Deputy. Ask me anything you want. Of course I'll do anything to help."

"You look prosperous enough."

The man shrugged, obviously surprised at the comment. "I have done fairly well, I must admit."

"So why in hell would you take a bribe to fiddle with a jury?"

Murphy stared at Longarm for a long moment. His face had paled at the abrupt accusation. Obviously stalling for time, he said, "You are referring, of course, to the trial of Wes Hardy."

"I am. Hardy has already admitted to me that he paid both you and Bill Rawlings to swing the jury."

"A bare-faced lie, as I am sure you must realize. What in tarnation would I need that man's money for?"

"Then you deny it?"

"Of course I deny it."

"Then why did you vote for acquittal?"

"Because it was obvious that I could not shake any of the other jurors. It was apparent from the beginning that Bill Rawlings had already decided how he was going to vote, and in addition, there was the matter of what would happen after the trial if Wes Hardy somehow got loose. The rest of the jurors were too frightened of this possibility to do anything that might arouse the man to move against them. He has a fearful reputation in these parts, Deputy. He threatened that he or his gang would take care of the whole jury."

Longarm involuntarily felt of his swollen jaw. It still hurt him some to blink his left eye. "So you went along."

"What choice had I? I have a spread to run. A man can delegate just so much responsibility, Deputy, and then things begin to fall apart. No matter how long I held out, it would have done no good."

"A hung jury might have forced another trial."

The man shrugged. "Deputy, what does it all matter

33

in the final reckoning? If Was Hardy was not hanged as a result of our jury's fecklessness, he will be hanged soon enough. A man like that courts hanging the way a whore does ruination."

Longarm did not know whether or not to believe the cattleman, but after what he had seen at the Rawlings's ranch, all he wanted was to stop the Calico Kid and let the devil take Wes Hardy for now. He sipped his drink. "I take it you are not living in fear of the Calico Kid."

"Why should I be, Deputy?"

"If we count Bill's death, he has already accounted for four of the jurors."

"Look about you, man. Is this the house of a peasant? I am surrounded by loyal men who would follow me to the brink because I treat them well. There are no lice in their bunks. They sleep between sheets that are freshly washed every week. Their food is plentiful and good. I have tacked no fool declarations about gambling on the walls of their bunkhouse. And when things are slow, I bring in women from Denver City to pleasure them. In short, Deputy, I take care of my men, and they take care of me."

"Or so you hope."

He leaned back. "Yes. So I hope. But, good Lord, man, none of us is designed to live forever."

"That had occurred to me."

"I assume you are after bringing in this Calico Kid. So what can I do to help you in this?"

"You can keep up your guard. I came to see you for two reasons—to follow up Hardy's charge that you had taken a bribe, and to alert you to the Kid's presence in the area."

Murphy laughed. "I believe I am more than ready for the Calico Kid. My men have already been told that the first one to bring him down will reap a thousand dollars and an expense-paid week in the fleshpots of Denver City."

Longarm's eyebrows went up as he considered the reward. This cattleman did indeed know how to treat his hands.

Murphy chuckled at Longarm's reaction. "As you can imagine, Deputy, it has more or less put them on the alert."

"I am glad I wasn't mistaken for the Calico Kid when I rode up to this compound."

"Deputy, by the time you were within ten miles of this compound you were being followed by two of my best men. I have it on their authority that you made your camp last night in Snake Draw, under the cottonwoods that bordered the stream. Am I correct?"

Longarm laughed. "You are."

The man got to his feet. "Find the Calico Kid, Deputy. He is a nuisance, to be sure. And watch out as well for that blackguard Wes Hardy. But, most important of all, remember that you have only to ask and I will give you whatever aid I can."

"I will need directions to get to the surviving members of that jury, Murphy. Perhaps one of your men could guide me."

"Let me see the list, if you will. I don't remember many of them."

Longarm dug the list out of his inside pocket and handed it to Murphy. The cattleman unfolded it and studied the names for a moment or so. Then he handed the list back to Longarm.

"The only one you'll have trouble finding is Ned Koerner. Jiggs Barney can take you to him. Ned's got a cabin in the foothills due west of here. I am sure Jiggs would be pleased to visit with his old sidekick for a spell. The two were prospectors together in California."

"Can you spare the man?"

"I can. Jiggs is getting a mite too old for ranch work, but I keep him around because he knows this country so well. He'll make an excellent guide, I assure you."

"Thank you."

Longarm got up and put his hat back on. Murphy rose also and escorted Longarm from the house. On the veranda, Longarm paused.

"Don't forget to send someone over to the Diamond K," he reminded the cattleman. "I don't like thinking of that woman alone there on that ranch, not with Wes Hardy on the loose."

Murphy smiled faintly. "I will do that, Deputy. But I know Joanna. She is a match for any eventuality. She will get along. Have no fear."

The owner spoke privately with his foreman for a while, then offered Longarm a chair beside him on the veranda. "Your guide will be here presently," he told Longarm.

Before long, a grizzled oldtimer wearing an immaculate shirt, Levi's, and tan Stetson rode up. He was leading a powerful black, already saddled with Longarm's saddle. Murphy explained that the black was a loan to Longarm and that he would pasture the mount Longarm had ridden in on.

Thanking Murphy, Longarm left the veranda and mounted the black.

As he took up his reins, he said, "There's just one thing I want to remind you of, Murphy."

"And what might that be, Deputy?"

"The Calico Kid does not have to wear a mask to kill

36

a man. In fact, that mask's a dead giveaway, and I am sure he knows it."

Murphy nodded serenely. "A good point, Deputy. I shall keep it in mind."

With Jiggs Barney at his side, Longarm pulled his mount around and rode out of the compound, heading for the sawtooth range that hung like a dark curtain in the sky.

That same day, Annie Reese entered Tillson's Emporium in Mills Falls. Approaching the counter with some trepidation, she waited patiently for Cal Rivkin, one of the owners, to wait on her.

"I need some material," Annie told Cal as soon as the man was free to wait on her. "It is for some... undergarments I am making." She blushed. "Do you have any silks?"

"Right this way, ma'am," said Cal, immediately taken with this pretty, blue-eyed woman who seemed so delightfully shy. "We have plenty of silks. Just off the boat from China, you might say."

"Really?" Annie exclaimed. "Just off the boat?"

"Hauled in from San Francisco this past week," Cal told her proudly. He stopped before a wall of large cubbyholes and began lifting down handsome silks. Annie exclaimed in delight at the soft textures and, after much consultation with Cal, made her purchase.

As Cal wrapped her silks, he leaned close to Annie and took a chance. "I am certain," he told her softly, "that this material will feel very nice against such a fair skin as yours."

Annie did not pull back. Instead, her eyes went warm as she smiled. "Oh, I'm sure it will. I can hardly wait! But, of course, nothing is as warm as a loving caress.

37

Don't you think so, Mr. Rivkin?"

Cal straightened up as if he had been struck. He had not expected such a straightforward reply to his advance. He had not expected it, but he was delighted, nevertheless. Almost too hastily he decided to follow up his advantage.

"Can I ... show you to your carriage?" he asked eagerly.

"Alas," said Annie, "I don't have one." Then she frowned down at the wrapped bundle. "My, these do look so heavy." She looked with pleading eyes at Cal. "I know this is a terrible thing to ask. I mean, you are so busy here. But would you consent to help me carry this heavy bundle to my room?"

"Where are you staying?" Cal asked, hardly daring to believe his luck.

In fact, he was having difficulty breathing. Though he was a happily married man, he had long since decided that one should never turn down a genuine invitation. And this was obviously the real McCoy. Something about him had taken this young delicacy's fancy. She had even troubled to learn his last name.

"I'm staying at the hotel," Annie responded, smiling with dazzling effect. "I just got in last night. Mills Falls is such a quiet place. I was so bored; and here I had been so looking forward to this shopping trip."

"You're ... staying alone, ma'am?"

"Yes, more's the pity. I could not get my Aunt Patricia to come with me on this trip."

"I'd be delighted to escort you, ma'am."

"Thank you. You are so kind."

"I'll just run back and tell my partner. It won't take long."

Smiling, Annie watched Cal Rivkin hurry off. Then,

still smiling, she walked to the front of the store to wait for him.

Cal's partner was Jim Tillson. Both he and Cal had served on the jury that had let Wes Hardy go free. Hardy had made it pretty clear to both of them during the trial that they would very likely lose their lives if they voted for conviction. Hardy rode with a tough bunch, and Hardy's men would see to it that those who had a hand in convicting Wes Hardy would suffer the consequences.

Still, despite the threat, it was only when it became obvious that Bill Rawlings and Howard Murphy were unshakable in their demand for acquittal that Jim had convinced Cal to go along with the rest of the jurors.

Now that it was all over and Wes Hardy had been freed to go his drink-sodden, violent ways, Jim Tillson felt not only shame at what he had done—but a bone-chilling fear, as well.

He felt shame because, as it turned out, Hardy's gang had fled as soon as Hardy had been arrested. Where they were now, no one knew. Hardy's threat, therefore, had been an empty one.

The fear Jim felt was for his life and Cal's. The Calico Kid had already killed three of the jurors. Though their deaths could have been the result of random shootings or attempted robberies, it sure as hell did not look that way.

And that was why he was worried now.

Three hours ago, Cal had come running back to tell him about this filly who had taken a shine to him. He had promised to be back within the hour, but here it was a full hour past closing time and there was no sign of him. It just wasn't like Cal to do such a thing.

Jim could wait no longer. Striding to the front of the store, he pulled down the shade, locked the door, then hurried out the rear of the store, locking that door as well. Cutting through the alley to the main street, he set sail for the town's only hotel. It was going to be rather indelicate if he barged in at the wrong time, Jim realized, but he was only thinking of Cal's safety.

The desk clerk smiled when he saw Jim. For a moment, Jim thought the cheeky youth was going to wink at him.

"Looking for Cal?" the clerk asked.

"Yes, I am," Jim responded, taken aback somewhat by the clerk's manner.

"Go right on up," the clerk said. "Cal told me to tell you he would be in room fourteen. That's the second floor, all the way back."

As Jim started up the stairs, the clerk could not resist piping out, "Have a good time! She's a real looker!"

Considerably nettled, but no longer worried about Cal's safety, Tillson mounted the stairs two at a time. At this rate, the entire community would know about Cal's indiscretions—and his, too, if that clerk babbled.

What could have gotten into Cal to make him confide so openly in the desk clerk? What in the world had come over Cal? It simply was not like him!

This observation stopped him in his tracks. He felt a sudden, sharp stab of fear deep in his gut. There was no doubt about it any longer.

Something was wrong!

Reaching the second floor, he proceeded down the dimly lit hallway. He found the door, his heart pounding, and knocked softly. He heard the squeak of bed springs as someone stood up.

"Yes?" The voice was that of a woman. It was soft and seductive. He heard her light footsteps approaching the door.

"Cal?" he asked. "Is Cal in there?"

"He's asleep," the woman whispered. She was so close to the door, he could hear her excited intake of breath as she went on. "I thought you'd never get here!"

The key turned in the lock and the door was pulled open. Jim gasped. The girl was standing in the open doorway completely naked—but that wasn't why he gasped. She was holding a Colt revolver in her hand. And behind her on the bed Jim saw the shiny face of Cal as he stared sightlessly up at the room's ceiling. Jim had seen death before, and in that instant he knew that Cal was dead.

But before he could turn and run, the girl had reached out and grabbed his arm. With a quick yank, she flung him into the room, then closed the door and locked it. Pulling up in front of the bed, Jim did not know whether to laugh or cry.

The girl was so beautiful, standing before him. In all his life he had never seen a woman so provocatively naked. As tall as he was, she stood straight and proud, her long golden hair curling about the nipples of her small, firm breasts, her pubic triangle a golden fleece of loveliness. Even her gently rounded belly was a delight to him.

"Take a look at me," she told him. "Take a good, long look. This is what you are going to lose when you die."

"My God! Who are you?"

"I am Carl Reese's daughter."

"Reese's daughter? He . . . he wasn't even married!"

"He was my father and he loved me and took care of me—sent me to a fancy school in San Francisco. He visited me whenever he could. Everything he could spare, he sent to me. I wanted for nothing. And when he was shot down in cold blood by Wes Hardy, you and the others on that jury cared not one whit. You let my father's murderer off. You let him off scot free!"

"Please! You don't understand! I had no choice— I—"

She did not let him finish. Striding close to the frantic man, she brought the barrel of her Colt down onto his skull with all the considerable force she could muster.

Jim Tillson remembered only an explosion of lights deep within the cavern of his mind. Then all the lights went out as he was whisked off into a roaring darkness.

As soon as it was dark, the Calico Kid opened the window and lowered to the back porch roof first Cal Rivkin and then Jim Tillson. Climbing out the window herself, she dropped a full story to the roof. Landing on cat feet beside the two stiffening bodies, she waited until she was certain the noise she had made had not alerted anyone. Then, looping her hangman's nooses around the necks of both men, she swung the bodies out into the alley, letting them fall to the ground behind her bay.

She took a deep breath and looked up the alley in both directions. A back door slammed shut in a building further down the alley. It was the restaurant, she knew, since she had studied this town for the past two weeks. Waiting for a minute or so longer, she dropped to the alley beside the two bodies, wound the ropes around her saddlehorn, and mounted up.

A few moments later, the startled citizens of Mills Falls heard the sudden roar of gunfire. Scrambling out of the saloons and those stores still open, they were just in time to see the Calico Kid, his sixgun blazing, come riding down the center of Main Street, dragging behind him the bodies of Cal Rivkin and Jim Tillson.

They were too astounded and too appalled to do anything but stare after the Calico Kid as he disappeared into the night. Then they broke for the two dead men he had left lying in the dust behind him.

Chapter 4

Jiggs Barney pulled up and pointed to a pine-covered ridge less than a mile ahead of them. "Ned's cabin is up there, Deputy. Behind them pines."

Longarm reined in his black. The sound of Jiggs's voice had startled him. This was only the second or third time during this interminable ride that his taciturn guide had spoken. The oldtimer was a dour prune of a man. He seemed to resent not only the errand his boss had sent him on, but the lawman he rode beside as well. To every attempt of Longarm's to break the ice, Jiggs Barney had muttered only the briefest of responses, until at last Longarm had given up.

Even more exasperating than his dour guide's silence was the poky, somewhat hesitant pace he maintained.

For a man who was supposed to know the country, Jiggs was not very impressive. At least three times they were forced to camp while Jiggs left him to study the terrain and decide in which direction they were to proceed. That they were finally close to reaching their destination was good news indeed to Longarm.

Longarm peered up at the ridge Jiggs had pointed out to him. "I hope that friend of yours has some hot coffee ready. I could use it."

Jiggs muttered something unintelligible and urged his mount on.

Soon they were riding up steep grades, and for the last hundred yards or so before they reached the ridge the going was exceedingly difficult. But Longarm's black managed beautifully. He was a fine, powerful animal, and Murphy's generosity in lending him to Longarm was greatly appreciated by the lawman.

Once they gained the ridge, it was a short ride to the pines. Approaching them, Longarm glimpsed the sagging roof and the raw, unpainted boards of the cabin's walls. Riding closer, a bit in front of Jiggs, he caught a sudden, furtive movement off to his right in among the pines.

Swiftly, Longarm reined in his mount.

It was a good thing he did. A rifle shot exploded from amongst the pines, the slug searing a hole through the air an inch or so above his head. Longarm flung himself from his saddle, dragging his Winchester from its scabbard as he did so. Behind him he heard Jiggs curse, and then the sound of the oldtimer's sixgun being cocked.

"Drop that rifle, Deputy," Jiggs told him coldly. "That was just a warning shot from Ned. The next time he'll put the slug where it belongs—right between your damned eyes."

Longarm looked back at Jiggs in bleak astonishment.

The old man was covering him with his revolver, a steely glint in his eyes. He still looked old and a mite worn, but all of a sudden he appeared to have developed the strength and durability of well-seasoned leather. Old Jiggs Barney was good for a long time yet to come.

"Drop the rifle," Jiggs repeated.

Longarm dropped the Winchester and turned to face Jiggs.

"Let's have that Colt you got under your coat," Jiggs told him. "Do it slow-like, and hand it up to me butt first."

Longarm reached across under his frock coat, took his .44 from its holster, and handed it to Jiggs. Jiggs tucked the Colt into his belt while he continued to cover Longarm with his sixgun. Behind him, Longarm heard Ned Koerner approaching through the brush. Before Longarm could turn, Ned jabbed the barrel of his rifle into the small of his back.

"He was too quick," said Ned to Jiggs, "or I would've had him."

"Dammit, Ned, didn't you get word? We ain't supposed to shoot him. We got to make it look like an accident."

"Howie's note just said to take the son of a bitch when he got here with you. Didn't say how I was to do it."

"Well, I'm telling you."

Longarm no longer needed an explanation for Jiggs's poky progress across the plains to these foothills. It was a deliberate and skillful strategem designed to give Howard Murphy's hard-riding messenger time to deliver that note to Ned.

"You two mind telling me what the hell is going on here? I'm looking for the Calico Kid. Are you and Murphy in cahoots with him?"

"Hell, we don't even know who he is," said Ned, grinning. "This here ain't got nothin' to do with that crazy varmint."

Ned was as dirty as Jiggs was clean. He wore a torn black floppy-brimmed hat, a filthy cotton undershirt, and patched britches. The boots he wore were held together with rawhide. Ned had only a few teeth left in his head and a white fuzz covered his cheeks. There was a raw, red look about his eyes, and his stomach had given up the good fight years ago and now hung far out over his think, broad leather belt. The rifle he was holding was an old Hawken.

"Let's go, Deputy," said Ned. "I got some coffee on."

"The condemned man ate a hearty meal—is that it?"

"Hell, I didn't say meal. I said coffee."

Jiggs exploded in laughter. Silently, Longarm followed Ned to his cabin. Jiggs, leading his and Longarm's mounts, came along behind.

The inside of the cabin looked as if a grizzly had just finished trashing it. The smell was powerful enough to curl Longarm's hair and, for a moment, he thought he was going to lose the jerky he had eaten that noon.

As soon as Jiggs stepped into the cabin after them, his face went white. "Jesus, Ned!" he exploded. "Ain't you cleaned this pigsty out yet?"

"I'm gettin' to it," Ned replied. "Next spring, maybe. What's the matter with you? It don't smell all that bad."

"That's because this stench has destroyed your damned nose!"

Wearily, Longarm sat down at the cluttered bench that served as a table. Jiggs sat across from him and rested his cocked weapon on the table in front of him, its muzzle pointing straight at Longarm.

Preferring to look away from the gaping muzzle,

Longarm took a long, unhappy look about him. The cabin had only two windows, with oiled paper serving as windowpanes. The light that managed to filter through cast a sickly, yellowish glow over everything. Sacks of flour, potatoes, and other foodstuffs were piled against one wall.

At the far end of the cabin, a filthy shambles of bedclothes sprawled atop an army cot served as Ned's sleeping quarters. Four chairs and the table at which they were sitting completed the furnishings. A noisome pile of unwashed dishes and pots and pans filled the corner of the cabin near the stove. The dirt floor was littered with rags, discarded clothing, broken crockery, empty whiskey bottles, and garbage.

But it was the source of the appalling smell that staggered Longarm. Apparently, whenever Ned was too cold or too lazy, he did not hesitate to relieve himself within the confines of his cabin. This would not have been so bad had he used a chamber pot. But Ned really did not have a pot to piss in, and from the corner he frequented came a stench so powerful it set Longarm's stomach to roiling.

It was with some relief that Longarm took the tin cup of steaming black coffee Ned set down before him. The coffee scalded him as it went down, but it was strong and filled him with some hope. When he finished it, he began chewing on the grounds that remained in the bottom of the cup. The grounds and the coffee were not much, considering this amounted to a condemned man's last meal, but it would have to do.

"Shall we get on with it?" Longarm asked.

Ned looked with some astonishment at Jiggs. "This here feller sure is in a hurry to die, ain't he?"

"He's just in a hurry to get out of this cesspool," Jiggs

responded, looking with some sympathy toward Long-arm. "That right, Deputy?"

"That's it," Longarm replied.

Ned Koerner leaned close. The stench of the man set Longarm's teeth on edge. "You are just goin' to have to hold your hosses, Deputy." Ned told him. "It ain't often I get visitors, and I ain't seen Jiggs here in a coon's age. So we'll just set here a spell and visit."

"Tell me," said Longarm, "how in blazes did you get the rest of the jurors to sit next to you during that trial?"

Ned grew sullen and pulled back.

It was Jiggs who answered. "Howie took care of that. Some of us Lazy M hands tied Ned up and took turns washing him. Took a while, it did. We used scrub brushes, plenty of hot water, and a good yellow soap. Ned howled like a stuck pig until we was finished with him. Then we shaved the poor slob, cut his hair, and gave him new clothes."

Ned looked shamefacedly at Longarm and nodded unhappily as he acknowledged the truth of Jiggs' account. "Couldn't barely stand it, I'm telling you," he said. "It didn't seem like it was me when they got done."

"What happened to your new clothes?"

"I'm wearin' 'em."

Longarm just shook his head. "Before you take me out and shoot me, I'd like a few answers."

"We ain't goin' to shoot you," said Jiggs.

"That's right. I forgot. You are going to make it look like an accident."

"Yes, sir, Deputy. That's what we got to do."

"And how do you plan to do that?"

Jiggs looked with a frown at Ned. "You got any ideas, Ned?"

"Nary a one."

"While you two make up your minds how to kill me, why not tell me the reason? What has Howard Murphy got to hide?"

Ned grinned at Longarm. "You see that big spread he's got? Do you know where he gets all that big money and all them cattle?"

Longarm shook his head.

"He *steals* it."

"What the hell does he need to do that for?"

"It's the easiest way, that's why. Since Howie gave up robbing banks and trains, he made himself respectable as a cattleman. His hands are the best and smartest bunch of rustlers and highwaymen in the West."

"I hate to admit it," said Jiggs, glancing with some pride at Longarm, "but what Ned here says is the God's truth. The Lazy M's hands are the slickest bunch of outlaws I ever saw collected in one place at one time." The old man fixed Longarm with his bright little eyes. "You ever hear tell of the Dooley Gang Massacre?"

Longarm frowned and thought back a moment. Then he remembered. "That was about ten years back, wasn't it? In Missouri?"

"That's where it was, all right."

"You were part of it?"

"Hell, I *planned* it. I'm Dooley. Leastways, I was then."

Longarm looked more carefully at the oldtimer. It was difficult for him to believe that this wiry old man had been the mastermind behind a raid that had wiped out nearly a quarter of the inhabitants of a small Missouri town, simply in order to relieve the local bank of its funds. By the time the town had recovered enough to alert the surrounding communities, the well-organized band had completely vanished.

"Learned my tactics with Quantrill," Jiggs said proudly. "He was a great teacher, he was."

"And, like you, a cold-blooded murderer."

Jiggs picked up his Colt and pointed it at Longarm. "That's right, Deputy. And don't you forget it."

"Just one more thing," said Longarm, pursuing a sudden hunch. "What did Murphy have to do with Carl Reese's death?"

"Hell," said Jiggs, "he's the one hired Wes Hardy to kill him. Reese was gettin' greedy. His price just got too high for him to look the other way when Wes brought in Murphy's 'mavericks'."

"So Hardy deliberately picked a fight with Reese, and then Murphy was lucky enough to be put on the jury that was to try his hired gunslick."

Jiggs grinned. "Sure was lucky, wasn't it?"

"Hey, Jiggs, I think I know how we can do it," said Ned. "Hangman's Ridge."

"You mean hang him?" Jiggs asked.

"Nope. We'll make it look like his horse got skittish and threw him off the ridge."

Jiggs beamed with pleasure at Ned's cleverness. "Why, that would be just the thing. And it sure as hell is a long way down, ain't it?"

"Yes, sir, it certainly is."

"We'd have to make sure we don't lose that black," Jiggs cautioned. "Howie said he's mine if I pull this off."

"Is that so? So what am *I* gettin'?"

"Enough gold to get you through the winter."

"Good old Howie," Ned said, brightening. "He never forgets his friends."

Jiggs nodded. "Just so long as you keep your distance."

"Now, Jiggs," complained Ned, "it warn't needed for you to say that."

"Just so you understand. You know the effect you have on the animals when you ride in."

Ned nodded unhappily. "Well, maybe I'll get me a washtub with this here money."

"You been threatening to do that for the last ten years," scoffed Jiggs.

Listening to these two old reprobates discussing his death and the proceeds to be wrung from the bloody enterprise, Longarm wondered if he had stumbled into a bad dream. But the stench was too powerful. No nightmare he had ever struggled though had boasted such an awesome smell.

"If you gents are settled on the matter of my demise," Longarm said, "I suggest we get on with it."

The two looked with some surprise at him.

"He sure is anxious, ain't he?" said Ned.

"Too anxious, I'm thinkin'," said Jiggs, frowning thoughtfully at Longarm. "Mebbe he's got somethin' up his sleeve."

"Like a weapon?" suggested Ned.

"It ain't that, dammit," protested Longarm. "It's the godawful smell in this place. I can't take much more of it."

Jiggs peered around at the noisome interior of the cabin. He took a quick, painful sniff and made a face. "You're right, Deputy. It is a fearful smell, and that's no lie. If Ned could bottle this stink, he could rid the world of skunks."

"Let's go," said Ned, his feelings dented only slightly. "Seein' as how this dude wants to get what's comin' to him sooner 'stead of later—ain't no reason we can't oblige him."

"Wait a minute," said Jiggs. "What you said before made sense. Maybe we better check this feller out once more. He's fancy enough to be wearin' a whore's gun, I'm thinking."

"Stand up," Ned told Longarm. "Real careful."

With a sigh, Longarm stood up. Ned spotted the gold chain instantly and with his filthy hand pulled the watch—and the derringer—from Longarm's vest pockets.

"Well, now," Ned crowed, holding up the timepiece. "Lookee what I found."

"You can have the watch," Jiggs said. "I'll take the derringer."

"I found them!" Ned protested. "They're both mine."

"Hell, we'll argue about it later," Jiggs said, snatching them out of Ned's hands and dumping them on the table. Longarm frowned as he saw the watch land heavily on the bench.

"Let me have his Colt then," said Ned. Without protest, Jiggs handed it to him.

Swiftly Jiggs pulled open the door and motioned with his revolver for Longarm to leave the cabin. Longarm did as he was directed and Jiggs followed out after him, still covering him. Longarm took a deep breath. It was glorious. Never in his life had fresh mountain air smelled so good.

The muzzle of Jigg's revolver jabbed him cruelly in the back. Longarm started toward the black.

"Hold it," said Jiggs. "If it's gonna look like an accident, we're gonna have to make sure his saddled mount runs into Bear Falls on the other side of the ridge. Word'll get around, and someone should come lookin' for him. But that way, I won't get the black, after all."

"That ain't no problem," said Ned. "Put his saddle on your horse and let the deputy ride the chestnut. You

54

can ride the black. That way you won't risk losing it."

"You'd better put my rifle in the scabbard too," Longarm told them. "And give me back my .44, still loaded. If that ain't on me when they find my body, they'll figure I was bushwhacked." He smiled at the two. "That means a whole passel of U. S. Deputies sniffing around these foothills looking for my murderer. The federal government don't like to lose any of its men."

"He's got a point," Ned told Jiggs.

"We'll give him back his weapons just before we pitch him over and spook his horse."

"Good idea."

Happy with their solution, Ned transferred Longarm's saddle to the chestnut Jiggs had been riding. Once the switch was complete, Jiggs mounted the black and told Longarm to get up onto the chestnut. As soon as Longarm did, Ned led his swaybacked mare out from the pines and climbed aboard. Longarm would not have believed it possible, but the mare smelled almost as bad as Ned.

"We'll follow you, Ned," said Jiggs.

They rode for close to a mile, going ever higher into the foothills. Soon the flanks of a great mountain materialized on their right and trail narrowed. It was only an hour or so before sundown when they reached Hangman's Ridge.

Jiggs had not exaggerated. It *was* a long way down.

"Get off your hoss, Deputy," said Jiggs.

Slowly, Longarm dismounted. Both men got off their mounts carefully, covering Longarm all the while.

"Don't forget," Longarm reminded them. "If you want this to look like an accident, you'll have to give me back that .44, fully loaded, and put the Winchester back in its scabbard, too."

Jiggs laughed. "Did you fall for that, Deputy?"

55

"Sure he did, Jiggs," cried Ned gleefully. "He really thought we'd give him back his arsenal before we killed him."

"We only let you think that to gentle you down some— to give you hope," Jiggs explained patiently to Longarm. "We always do that when we're going to kill someone. Works every time."

"We'll flatten your skull somewhat," Ned went on happily. "Then is when we'll give you back your loaded .44 and roll you over the edge. After that we'll put your Winchester back in its saddle sling and spook the chestnut."

"My horse will probably find its way back to your cabin, Ned," Longarm said hopefully. "That would be a dead giveaway."

"No, it won't. We'll make sure it's on its way to Bear Falls before we spook it."

Longarm sighed. "Then I guess this is it."

Both men moistened their lips and nodded.

Turn around, Deputy," said Jiggs.

"No," said Longarm.

As he said this, he took a step toward them.

"Now, listen here," insisted Jiggs. "There ain't no sense in you coming at us now. You ain't got no chance. No chance at all."

"If you shoot me, it won't look like an accident," Longarm pointed out, smiling meanly. "So you are going to have to take me without firing a shot."

"See that?" said Ned, glancing unhappily at Jiggs. "I knew it! Let's just shoot the son of a bitch and bury his body."

"Dammit, Ned, we are going to do this right. You go on around behind him. When I give the word, both of us will come at him."

"Aw, shit," grumbled Ned. "I knew this wasn't going to be as easy as it looked."

"You old woman!" snapped Jiggs. "Move!"

Longarm tensed and waited. As soon as Ned was out of his line of sight, he flung himself at Jiggs. Jiggs saw him coming and tried to bring his sixgun down on Longarm's head. Longarm slammed into Jiggs's mid-section just as the barrel of Jigg's Colt glanced off his skull. It hurt some, but not enough to deter Longarm.

His feet digging into the ridge's thin soil, he drove Jiggs back until the old man went down under him. Longarm make no effort to cushion Jiggs from the effects of his considerable heft. Jiggs grunted painfully as the air was expelled from his lungs. Longarm could not be sure, but he thought he heard one of the old man's ribs crack.

Snatching the Colt from Jiggs's hand, he rolled over, cocked it, and fired up at the charging Ned. But the shot went wild. Ned kicked the gun out of his grasp, then kicked Longarm viciously in the side. The tip of Ned's boot dug deeply and painfully into his kidney. Ignoring the pain, he grabbed Ned's boot and twisted, bringing the old man down hard.

But by this time Jiggs had regained his feet and was rushing him. Longarm heard Jiggs coming, rolled away, and snatched up the weapon Ned had kicked out of his hand. Jiggs flung himself on Longarm and tried to keep him down until Ned could help him out. But the old man was no match for Longarm's strength. Twisting free with a violent wrench, Longarm brought up the revolver, cocked it, and sent a round into Jiggs's belly.

"Oh, Jesus," Jiggs said as he rolled over on the ground, both hands clutching at the streaming hole in his gut.

Longarm turned around, looking for Ned. He was too

late. Swinging Longarm's Winchester like a club, Ned caught the lawman on the back of his head. It staggered Longarm and he went sprawling forward, his senses reeling. But he was not out completely and, rolling over, he swung the revolver up and fired at Ned. The slug caught Ned high in the left shoulder, knocking him back. Clutching at his shoulder, Ned went down on one knee, his eyes wide with the pain.

Longarm climbed shakily back up onto his feet. His head was still ringing from the blow he had sustained. Then, from behind him, came a terrifying scream. It was wrung, it seemed, from the very bowels of hell. Longarm spun around. Though Jiggs Barney was now a dead man, in his rage he had managed somehow to lurch back onto his feet and charge Longarm. Before Longarm could dodge aside, the old man had slammed head first into his midsection.

The force of Jiggs's charge rocked Longarm back toward the edge of the ridge. He was dealing now with the fury of an old campaigner, and though he was much stronger than Jiggs, he found Jiggs's charge irresistible. He kept trying to dig in his heels—until there was no longer any place to put his feet down.

Locked together in fierce embrace, the two men toppled off the ridge.

As the uneven ground slammed into Longarm's back, he felt Jiggs's body launch itself into space and fly on past him. As he fell, Jiggs screamed. Still on his back, Longarm scrabbled frantically for something to catch hold of. A boulder slammed into Longarm's back, slowing him down. He caught hold of a clump of juniper and slowed himself still more. With a hard, violent whack, his back slammed into the trunk of a small pine. Wrapping both arms about the gnarled tree, he hung on.

As soon as he could manage it, he glanced up at the brow of the ridge. He could not see either the ridge or the pines topping it.

"Deputy!" Ned Koerner called.

Longarm did not reply.

"You're a dead man, Deputy! Damn your hide! I'll be up here waitin' on you."

Longarm took a deep breath and closed his eyes. He needed time to regain his wits and gather what strength still remained. After a minute had passed, he glanced down at the yawning chasm below him. Where Longarm clung to the side of the cliff, it was not yet dusk. In the chasm below, however, it was already night, and the river that snaked through it looked from this height no wider than a girl's hair ribbon.

As soon as he was strong enough, Longarm began his journey back up the slope to meet the waiting Ned. He moved like an enormous worm, his body absorbing every sound, every loose patch of dirt or gravel. Climbing steadily, with infinite patience, he refused to move higher until he was absoultely certain each time that he was not going to dislodge any rocks. When finally he pulled himself up onto the ledge, it was pitch dark.

He looked around. The moon had not yet risen above the mountains. But Longarm did not need his eyes. His sense of smell would do just as well—perhaps even better.

On his hands and knees, he moved away from the edge, his nose up, sniffing like a hound dog at the damp mountain air. Then he caught Ned's awesome stench. He spun to his right. Out of the night came the old man, lumbering painfully. Longarm jumped up to meet the wounded old man's charge. The two slammed together. Ned's smell made Longarm feel sick, but he fought down

59

his nausea and grabbed at his .44 which Ned clutched in his grimy hand. They struggled for the weapon. It went off. A searing pain ripped at Longarm's side, but he did not release his hold on the barrel.

With a sudden, vicious wrench, he twisted the gun free and clubbed the old man to the ground. But Ned was not finished. He reached up and grabbed at Longarm, who pulled away, kicking out viciously, catching Ned under his ribs. The old man lifted, rolled over, and kept going as he plunged—as silent as a rock—into the chasm.

Longarm stuck his .44 back into his rig and turned to look for his horse. But his head seemed to be spinning off his shoulders. The ground tipped up violently and cracked him on the side of the head.

The sun's unblinking eye was peering over the horizon, drilling a hole in his forehead. Longarm turned his face away from it and began to crawl toward a small patch of shade. It took him an eternity to reach the shade, and night fell before he made it.

Throughout the night he shivered violently, his teeth chattering like castanets. Dawn came again, and this time Longarm glimpsed the chestnut cropping grass on the trail below the ridge. He crawled over to get his Winchester and then continued on his hands and knees toward the horse. He reached the animal and managed to catch its reins with one desperate swipe. The flanks of the animal were slick with his blood before he was able to pull himself up into the saddle. Leaning forward with his head on the horse's neck, he urged it on back down the trail.

It was almost noon when Longarm reached Ned's cabin. He slid off the horse, went inside the cabin, and found a jug of water. He gulped its contents down swiftly before he realized he was drinking moonshine. It seared his gullet and burned into his gut like kerosene. Longarm slumped into one of the chairs, saw his derringer and watch, and, fumbling blearily, dropped them into his vest pockets.

He knew that he had to do something about the hole in his side. It was not deep, but blood was streaming out of it. This, together with the moonshine, had left him feeling not only light-headed, but positively drunk.

Yet, even in his state, he was not insensible to the awesome stench of Ned's cabin. He staggered out the door and collapsed on the ground, rolled over just once, and closed his eyes. He would probably bleed to death, he knew. But he sure as hell was not going to do it in that pigsty.

Longarm stirred fitfully. The side of his face was resting on something warm and yielding. Deliciously warm and deliciously yielding. He became aware of a woman's arms pulling him closer to her. He opened his eyes and found himself looking up into a woman's face. She was smiling down at him the way a mother would smile at the babe at her breast.

They were both lying on a bed, and she was completely naked. Except for the bandage wrapped tightly around his waist, so was he.

"I knew you weren't dead," she told him, hugging him still closer. "But you would have been if I hadn't done this. Do you mind?"

"No," Longarm managed. "I don't mind. Who...are you? How long have I—"

"Shh. Don't fret. My name is Annie. You're in my cabin. I found you in the mountains. By the time I got you here, you were very cold and very still."

Longarm managed a grin. "I'm warming up now," he told her. "Fast."

She laughed, a warm, soft laugh that filled him with a sudden rush of desire for her. "That's fine. I've got some broth on the stove. Let me get it for you."

He watched her as she swung off the bed and walked from the bedroom. She had long blonde hair that went almost clear to her waist. Her body was as slim as a boy's, but there was nothing masculine in the way she moved or in the pert fullness of her small breasts.

He was almost willing to believe he really had died— and gone to heaven.

Chapter 5

Howard Murphy left the blacksmith shop as soon as he heard his foreman calling his name. Stepping out into the bright sunlight, he pulled the brim of his hat down to shield his eyes.

Gil Dugan was hurrying across the compound leading the black—the one Murphy had told Jiggs he could keep if he finished off that deputy. It was still saddled, but Jiggs was nowhere in sight. That meant trouble. Murphy could feel it in his bones, and he didn't like the feeling. Perhaps he should not have given a job this important to a couple of old fools like Jiggs Barney and Ned Koerner. Maybe he should have taken care of that deputy himself.

Gil pulled up in front of him, patting the black's neck

to quiet him. The big animal was still a mite skittish. Dry flecks of foam clung to his flanks and his eyes were wild and staring. "He's come all the way back alone," Gil said.

Murphy nodded. "I knew something was wrong when Jiggs didn't show up this morning."

"What'll we do, Howie?"

"Saddle up. We got a ride ahead of us. I'd like Red and Jeeter to come with us."

Gill nodded and led the horse away toward the horse barn. Watching him go, Murphy took a deep breath. He hadn't liked the looks of that deputy U. S. marshal. He was lean and tough, with the resilience of good leather, and no man's fool. Sure—and this lathered horse was proof enough of that.

He glanced up at the sun. They should reach Ned's cabin about an hour before sunset.

The next day, close to sundown, Joanna Rawlings was returning to the cabin with an empty swill bucket when she caught sight of a growing dust cloud. Shielding her eyes, she peered into the shimmering distance until she was able to recognize the leading rider. It was Howard Murphy, with four Lazy M riders at his back. Hastily brushing an errant lock of hair off her forehead, she hurried for the cabin.

"Wes!" she called. "It's Murphy and four of his riders. And they're riding hard!"

Wes met her in the doorway. He was wearing no shirt, and his entire upper torso was swathed in bandages. He did not appear to be in any discomfort, however, as he stepped out of the doorway past Joanna to look for himself.

He watched the approaching riders for a moment, then

turned back to her. "It's Howie, all right. I wonder what he wants."

A couple of days before, after learning of Bill Rawlings's death from that deputy U. S. marshal, Murphy had sent two riders to check on Joanna. They had obviously been surprised to see Wes so clearly at home with Rawlings's widow, but had said nothing and ridden promptly back to the Lazy M after Joanna filled their bellies with hot biscuits and coffee.

The riders were closer now, and there was something in the way that Murphy rode his horse and the grim look of his riders that warned both of them that this time it was trouble, not curiosity, that had brought them company. Remembering what he had admitted to that deputy, Wes felt more than a little uneasy.

Joanna glanced at him, a troubled frown on her face. "You got any idea what they want?"

"Hell, no. But remember, it was the Calico Kid killed Bill."

Joanna nodded grimly. "Don't worry. They'll never learn the truth from me."

The five riders did not let up when they reached the compound. Only when they were a few feet from Wes and Joanna did they pull up, their faces hard. Dust and grit raised by their horses swirled about the two. Squinting painfully, Joanna dug at her eyes to get the gritty sand out of them. When she looked back up, she saw Murphy and his four riders forming a circle around them.

"What the hell is this, Howie?" Wes demanded, squinting up through the dust. "You tryin' to rile me?"

"Maybe, Wes. You sure as hell rile me."

"Now what's that supposed to mean?"

"You blabbed to that deputy, didn't you?" he asked harshly. "You spilled your guts to the son of a bitch—

and now he's gone and killed Jiggs and Ned. I hold you responsible."

"What the hell are you talkin' about?"

"You denying you told him you bought me and Bill Rawlings off? You denying you told him Bill and I was paid by you to hold that jury in line?"

Wes blinked unhappily up at Murphy. "The son of a bitch had already shot me. I was bleedin' like a stuck pig. He acted like he was looking forward to pulling that trigger again."

"You're going to wish he had, boy. It was bad enough you told him you knew me. You had to make him think you could buy me as well."

"Hell, Howie! I just wanted to get him off my back so I could take him later on. I figured he'd come out here lookin' for Bill, so I headed out here to wait for him. And if he came to your place first, I figured you'd know what to do with him."

"You put him onto me, Wes. I told you never to point the law at me or my boys here. I paid you well to kill Reese, and Rawlings got a nice piece of change for keeping the rest of those jurors in line—but the killings have brought in a federal deputy—a tough son of a bitch who has already killed Jiggs and Ned, and who now knows I want him dead." Murphy looked long and hard at Hardy. Then, his voice low, his eyes colder than death, he said, "You owe me, Wes."

Wes moved uncomfortably under those eyes. "The hell I do."

"You heard me. And I intend to see that you pay in full."

"There ain't no use you threatening me, Murphy," Wes snapped angrily. "You know better than that."

Murphy glanced at Gil Dugan. The foreman nodded,

glanced at his men, and dismounted. The three Lazy M hands dismounted also. They approached Hardy cautiously.

"Stand aside, Joanna," Murphy told the woman, "and keep out of this."

Without a word of protest, Joanna moved swiftly to one side. She seemed bemused, her eyes watching Wes without a glimmer of concern.

The four Lazy M hands pounced on Wes. Not having completely recovered from his two wounds, the scuffle was a short and painful one for Hardy. As soon as Wes was completely subdued, Murphy unwound a bullwhip from his saddlehorn and dismounted.

Measuring his distance carefully, he nodded to his hands. They stepped to one side. The bullwhip whistled through the air, snapping with a mean crack about Hardy's bandaged chest. With a furious oath, Hardy tried to pull away. Murphy yanked cruelly, his short, blocky body exhibiting rock-solid strength. Wes staggered and fell to one knee. Flipping his wrist, Murphy uncoiled the whip from around Hardy.

Wes lurched to his feet, loosing a string of black oaths at Murphy. With a short, mean laugh, Murphy uncoiled his whip and once again sent it through the air. It sounded like a rifle shot as it snapped cruelly around Hardy's bandaged chest. Again and again, Murphy lashed at Wes until the man's bloodied bandages hung from his torso like strips of flesh. At last Wes collapsed, groaning, to the ground, but Murphy continued to chastise him until finally, breathing heavily, he flipped the whip free and nodded once more to his men.

Swiftly they closed about Hardy and began to punish him, using their boots as well as their fists. When they stepped back, they were panting heavily. Blood trickled from one corner of Wes's mouth and one eye was already purpling.

"Stand up, Wes!" Murphy snapped. His voice was almost as sharp as the crack of his whip.

Slowly, doggedly, Wes got to his feet. Sucking in huge gulps of air, he glared in silence at his tormentor.

"That deputy you sent after me is still out there," Murphy told him. "He has killed Jiggs and Ned. I want you to find him and kill him. Until you do, Wes, your account with me will not be closed. Is that clear?"

For a moment, Wes hesitated, but only for a moment. "I'll get the son of a bitch, Murphy," he said. Then, licking his puffy lips, he threw his powerful shoulders back. "And after that, maybe I'll come looking for you."

"You do that, Wes," Murphy said, grinning as he slowly rewound his whip. "The welcome mat is always out for friends of the Lazy M." He glanced around him at his men. "Is that not correct?"

The four riders nodded solemnly.

Murphy glanced over at Joanna. As he appraised her slim, erect bearing, his ruddy face softened. "It wasn't the Calico Kid shot your husband. It was Wes Hardy. Am I right, Joanna?"

She nodded.

"You can do better than Wes. Come stay at the Lazy M for a while. It could use the touch of a strong woman." He smiled. "And then, I've always admired the Diamond K spread. It is prime grazing land."

Joanna said, "I'll get my things."

"No need for that, Joanna. We'll just ride into Denver City soon and see about your new wardrobe." Murphy turned to Gil. "Saddle up a mount for Joanna."

A few minutes later, a battered, sullen Wes Hardy stood in the cabin doorway and watched Joanna ride off with Howard Murphy and the Lazy M riders. Yes, he sure as hell had a good reason to find and kill that deputy—but the account that interested Hardy the most was the one he now had to settle with Howard Murphy.

But first things first. There was a jug of moonshine under the sink. He would empty it, lick his wounds for a while, and set out after that goddamned deputy.

Turning painfully, Wes Hardy disappeared into the cabin.

Annie smiled contentedly up at Longarm. "My," she said. "You're all better. I can tell."

They were lying on the bed side by side, naked. A small bandage was all that was required now to cover Longarm's wound. Annie placed one of Longarm's big hands over her breast. The late afternoon sun slanted in through the window, planting a golden trapezoid on the bedroom wall.

"If I am," Longarm told her, "I have you to thank, Annie."

"Well, you are—and you're welcome." Clasping her hand over his, she sighed. "I suppose this means you'll be moving out now."

He pulled himself closer and, holding her small breast more firmly, turned her gently toward him. "Yes, Annie. There are five members of that jury still alive—no thanks to me. I've got to stop the Calico Kid before he reduces that number to four."

He kissed her. Her mouth softened under his probing lips and then opened. He felt himself coming to life again. His mouth still working over hers, he pulled her hard against him. With a tiny, mischievous cry, she flung one leg over his thigh. On fire by this time, he reached down with his big right hand and swiftly drew her small, firm buttocks under him.

Entering her moist warmth effortlessly, he began to move, slowly at first, savoring each delicious stroke, his hand pressing her up into him. It took a while for him to build to his climax, but Longarm did not mind. Good times like this always went too fast. He smiled down at her as he felt himself reaching his climax. Her fingernails dug into his shoulders. The pain was so intense it almost rivaled the fire building in his groin. Then, with a sudden, happy cry they clung to each other, shuddering in ecstatic unison.

Sadly, inevitably, the sweet closeness was over. They uncoupled. Gently, he kissed her on the cheek, then on both eyelids.

"You see," she whispered. "Like I said. You are now as good as new."

"Better."

She looked at him unhappily. "When will you leave?"

"First thing tomorrow morning."

She snuggled closer. "It has been so nice, Longarm. Do you think you'll ever ride back this way again?"

"Like I told you, I got some fool jurors to see to and the Calico Kid to apprehend."

"Suppose the Calico Kid just disappears?"

Longarm frowned. "He could, I suppose. No one knows who he is or where he comes from."

"He might, then."

Longarm laughed gently. "That's just wishful thinking. Even if he were to disappear, I still have a few things to settle with one very smooth gentleman, Howard Murphy. Not only was he the one who hired Wes Hardy to kill Reese, the son of a bitch tried to have me killed, too." He looked speculatively at Annie for a minute, almost as if he were seeing her for the first time. "But I tell you what, Annie—if I manage to live through all

that, you can bet I'm coming back. I've just about decided it's time for this lawman to settle down."

Annie sat up suddenly in the bed. Brushing her blonde
hair out of her eyes, she asked eagerly, "Do you really
mean that, Longarm?"

"Sure. Why not? You've got a nice horse farm here.
Beef cattle I got no hankering to wet-nurse. But horses
are different. And from the looks of things, I think you
need a man around here."

She leaned forward and kissed him warmly and happily. He kissed her back, as surprised as she was at this
astonishing declaration of his—and just as pleased as
she was that he had had the good sense to make it.

It was with a clearer head the next day that Longarm
realized he had spoken a mite foolishly to Annie. The
intoxicating warmth of her arms had undoubtedly been
responsible for his lapse. He sensed that Annie knew
this, and understood. So neither of them said a word
about it, and when at last Longarm was ready to mount
up, he simply kissed her gently and thanked her for
everything.

He had already told her where he was heading next.
Again, she warned him about Pete Bergstrom.

"He's an old bear," she insisted. "I think he's half
mad. Let the Calico Kid go after him. He might kill the
Kid."

Longarm laughed. "Maybe. But I don't have any
choice, Annie. I have to warn him, at least."

She sighed, went up on tiptoe to kiss him, then stepped
back as he mounted the chestnut.

He touched the rim of his cap to her, wheeled his
horse, and rode out. Topping a distant ridge, he glanced
back at the cabin. Annie was standing in the doorway.

He waved. She waved back. A curious ache arose in his throat, and he wondered if perhaps he was not getting too old and maybe just a mite too foolish for this line of work.

Pete Bergstrom's mountain farm was a shambles. It had never been anything else. The woman he had purchased in a Colorado Springs saloon had stayed for less than a fortnight, and since that shrill disaster, he had made no effort at all to keep up the place.

There were three buildings in all—a small, unpainted cabin, a sagging barn, and the remains of a lean-to shed— enclosed in a rectangle of rotting fence posts, the cross members having long since fallen away and disintegrated. Tree stumps pocked the front yard, and scattered about between them were pieces of a broken wagon wheel, a rusted bedspring, and a whetstone, no longer functional as it lay on its side, broken and overgrown.

But this was all Pete Bergstrom had. It was his home, his castle, scratched out of thin, rocky soil on the lip of a narrow plateau flanked by the sides of great mountains. He was content, and bound and determined to protect himself and his farm from the Calico Kid or any other stranger who threatened him and his bleak, solitary world. It had been bad enough that he had had to serve on that jury. But it had taught him a lesson. He would never again let anyone take him away from his place.

He pulled the cabin door shut and picked his way across his littered front yard, heading for the saddled swaybacked mule waiting in front of the barn. A ragged flock of chickens fluttered and squawked as he strode through their midst, but he paid them no heed. Bergstrom had returned to his cabin to replenish his supplies, and was now on his way back to his lookout, a high perch that gave him an unobstructed view of the trail leading up to his spread.

He would not even have known of the Calico Kid's menace, but he had gone to Mills Falls a few days before and heard talk of the way the bloody carcasses of Jim Tillson and Cal Rivkin had been dragged down Main Street by the Kid. Everyone knew the Kid's purpose by this time: to kill every member of the jury that had let Wes Hardy off. So, as soon as Bergstrom rode into town, a small crowd had gathered to jabber excitedly at him, anxious to see the solitary old codger's reaction. They were disappointed. Bergstrom had listened impassively, ascertained to his satisfaction that they were telling him no more than the truth, then spat and strode into the general store to purchase his goods.

The only difference their chilling account of the Calico Kid's depredations made on Bergstrom's plans was the addition he made to his list of purchases: a fresh box of center fire cartridges for his Sharps. And this was apparent only to the clerk who waited on him.

Mounting the sad-looking swaybacked mule, Bergstrom rode off. It was a little past noon, and sun caused him to pull the torn brim of his black hat down to shield his eyes. He reached his post without incident and settled down behind the boulder he had selected. When he pushed his hat back up off his forehead he caught the glint of sunlight on metal and saw a horse and a rider toiling up the trail toward him.

Swiftly he reached for the forked stick he was using as a stand and thrust it into the ground. He cursed silently. The rider was now less than three hundred yards away. If he had caught sight of him earlier, he could have stopped the rider long before he had gotten this close. Swiftly slipping a shell into the Sharps' chamber, he pulled the hammer back gently, tucking the stock securely into his shoulder, and squeezed the trigger.

A chunk of ground in front of the rider's chestnut flew into the air. For a moment, the hapless rider had to contend with a frantic, rearing animal. Bergstrom levered out the empty brass shell, reloaded, and placed another round at the horse's feet. This time the rider did not try to stay in the saddle. He leaped from the animal's back, hauling his rifle out of its scabbard as he dashed up through the rocks toward Pete Bergstrom.

Cursing, Bergstrom tried to get a bead on him, but the son of a bitch kept his head down as he continued to move forward. Losing sight of him for a longer period than usual, he lifted himself higher and caught the glint of a rifle barrel. He ducked just as the rifle below him cracked, sending a round whining off a boulder beside him. As the tiny shards of rock showered him, Bergstrom plucked his forked stick out of the ground and retreated higher into the rocks. He knew this mountainside as well as he knew the cracks in his cabin ceiling, and it was not long before he was well out of range of the Calico Kid.

For Berstrom was certain it was the Kid he was battling. Who else but the Calico Kid would be foolish enough to continue on in the face of his Sharps? This was not the first time Bergstrom had warned away intruders in this fashion. Never before had anyone continued on after his warning fire sprayed the ground before them.

Bergstrom's mind was made up. The next time he set himself, he would shoot to kill.

As Longarm clambered up through the rocks, he remembered Annie's warning and shook his head ruefully. She had certainly been right. This fellow Bergstrom was a wild one, for sure. He obviously owned a Sharps and was using it with great skill.

So what in tarnation was he doing chasing the poor crazy bastard? Why didn't he just turn his back on him and ride the hell out of here? Hell, like Annie said, he was crazy enough to stop the Calico Kid without any help from Longarm. Why not let him?

He pulled up, flung his head back, and called out Bergstrom's name. It echoed and reechoed among the rocks. Longarm waited a while and called out a second time, warning the man that he was a law officer. But when the echoes died, there was no reply from the hidden sodbuster. Shrugging wearily, Longarm pulled himself up past a stunted juniper, hoping to get close enough to Bergstrom to talk some sense into him.

From far, far above him in the rocks, the Sharps cracked hollowly, the long, rolling echo coming a split second after the rock just above Longarm's head exploded. Instantly, fresh rivulets of blood streamed down over his forehead as the clawing shards of stone riddled his hat and cut through his scalp. Cursing in frustration, Longarm flung himself down and proceeded to mop off his bloody forehead.

He did not need this, he told himself bitterly as he dabbed at his riddled forehead. No, he did not. To hell with the Calico Kid! This crazy sodbuster was the real threat around here. Longarm was damned if he was going to let him get away with sniping at a deputy U. S. marshal.

Bergstrom had seen the Calico Kid go down. Peering over the lip of the rock just below him, he caught a glimpse of the Kid. He was hatless, and blood was

75

streaming down over his forehead. Bergstrom jumped up and begun to clamber swiftly down the slope.

He had wounded the Calico Kid. Hellfire! He would bring the murdering son of a bitch in on the end of a rope, just the way the Kid had brought in Rivkin and Tillson. He was too excited to realize that not once had he glimpsed any sign of the calico bandanna drawn up over the Kid's face—the Calico Kid's trademark, as every single observer had pointed out.

Longarm heard Bergstrom clambering down the rocks toward him. He did not want to kill the foolish bastard. But if the trigger-happy idiot didn't listen to reason, Longarm would have no choice.

Clapping his hat back on, he turned to look up the slope. Bergstrom popped into view. For a split second, the two men stared at each other—less than twenty yards separating them—before Bergstrom ducked behind a boulder.

"Bergstrom!" Longarm called. "You're firing on a U.S. marshal! Stop it, you crazy old coot, or I'll bring you in!"

"You can't fool me! You're the Calico Kid!"

"Like hell I am! Where's my calico bandanna?"

"If you're not the Calico Kid, what're you doin' here?"

"Dammit, I came to warn you. I'm after the Kid myself."

"Well, he ain't here, and I'm already warned. So turn around and get out of here!"

Longarm sat back on his haunches and scratched his head. Damned if the old coot didn't make sense, at that. There was no question this mountain-bound sodbuster knew how to handle that Sharps of his.

"All right!" Longarm cried. "I'll go back."

"Go on, then!"

Longarm stood up slowly, turned, and picked his way cautiously back down the way he had come. Glancing back, he saw the oldtimer perched on a ledge, his rifle at his shoulder, covering him as he went. Longarm didn't like it, and was tempted to tell the man to put down the Sharps. He thought he could feel its muzzle pressing a hole between his shoulder blades and was expecting at any moment to hear the sudden roar of its detonation.

But the shot, when it came, was a more distant report. As the crackling echo rolled about the rocks, Longarm spun to see Bergstrom collapsing forward, his Sharps clattering to the ground at his feet.

"Son of a bitch!" Longarm gasped as he clambered up onto the flat face of a boulder that gave him a view of the trail.

He was not surprised at what he saw. Once again he was watching the Calico Kid galloping away from another assassination. Sweeping off his hat, he slapped his thigh in exasperation. For a moment he considered racing back down the slope to his horse and taking after the Kid, but he knew from experience how small a chance he had of overtaking that bay the Kid rode.

Jumping down from the rock, he moved cautiously on up the slope toward the wounded sodbuster. It was a good thing he was careful, because as Longarm got to within six feet of him, the grizzled oldtimer snatched up his Sharps and tried to get off a shot.

Longarm kicked the rifle out of his hands, then bent to see how badly Bergstrom was hurt.

"Damn your hide," Bergstrom growled, baring his yellow teeth. "I shoulda knowed you was in cahoots with that killer."

"Shut up," snapped Longarm wearily. "Let me see how bad you're hurt."

Grumbling, Bergstrom allowed Longarm to examine him. He was in considerable pain, but said nothing as Longarm rolled him over and found a ragged hole in his lower back. A steady gout of blood was pulsing from the wound, and it looked as if the old man's right hip had been shattered as well.

Longarm stood up, frowning, then came to a quick decision. He ripped Bergstrom's shirt off and wound it around his waist in an attempt to stop the blood flowing from the back wound. It was some help, but not much.

Ignoring the sodbuster's sudden yelp of pain, he picked Bergstrom up and carried him down the treacherous slope to his waiting mount. Bergstrom was still conscious when Longarm slung him over the saddle and led his horse up the trail toward the distant plateau. Not long after, however, his blood pulsing down over the flanks of the chestnut, Bergstrom passed out.

When Longarm lifted Bergstrom down off his horse and carried him into his cabin about half an hour later, he could tell that the sodbuster was not going to make it. No man could lose as much blood as he had and stay alive. Gently, Longarm placed the old man down on his narrow cot.

Bergstrom's eyes flickered, then opened. When he saw Longarm, he frowned. "You ain't in cahoots with the Kid?"

"I told you. I'm a lawman."

"Well, you sure as hell didn't do me any good. I'm a dead man."

Longarm nodded unhappily in agreement.

"You from Denver City?" the oldtimer asked.

"That's right, old man."

"Look up my boy. Tell him he can have this spread if'n he wants it."

"What's his name?"

"William Clancy Bergstrom. He ain't worth much. I kicked him out when he got too old to mind. He runs a livery stable near the rail yards."

"I'll tell him."

"It's the least you can do," Bergstrom snapped.

The old man closed his eyes. Longarm leaned closer, studied his pale, waxen features for a long moment, then took a deep breath.

Bergstrom was dead.

Chapter 6

It was a very discouraged Longarm who rode into Annie's yard a little before sundown. Annie, carrying a water bucket, appeared in the barn doorway, a smudge on her chin, her hair in some disarray. She appeared momentarily startled at his unheralded appearance. Then her face broke into a wide grin as she hastily set down the water bucket and ran across the yard to greet him.

Dismounting wearily, Longarm turned in time to catch her as she threw herself into his arms.

"Whoa, there, Annie," he cautioned as she planted an enthusiastic kiss on his cheek. "I didn't come here to celebrate any kind of a victory. I came back to lick my wounds."

Frowning suddenly, she stepped back from him to get a better look. "But you are fine," she said. "There's no sign of blood. You have no wounds that I can see."

"Pete Bergstrom is dead."

She stepped closer, sudden concern on her face. Taking him gently by the arm, she asked, "Did you get there too late?"

"I got there in plenty of time," Longarm replied wearily. He looked past her at the cabin. "You got any fresh coffee on?"

"I have indeed."

"I need some—and then maybe something a little stronger."

"Then will you tell me what happened?"

"Yes. Then I'll tell you what happened."

As Longarm strode beside Annie into the cool interior of her cabin, he could not help reflecting how good it felt to be back here with Annie, especially when he eased his big frame into the familiar chair at the deal table and watched her hurry over to the stove to fetch his coffee.

It was almost like coming home.

But he put that reflection firmly out of his mind as he sipped the black brew and watched Annie place a half-full bottle of rye down before him on the table. It wasn't Maryland rye, but it would do. Annie sat down across from him and rested her face in both hands as she watched him drink the coffee, then pour some whiskey into the cup. He downed the whiskey in one gulp.

Winking at her, Longarm took out a cheroot, lit it, and leaned back in the chair, somewhat guilty all of a sudden that he could feel this good.

"You do know how to take care of a man," he told Annie, filling the air above his head with smoke from his cheroot.

"You feel better now?"

"I do indeed."

"I'll make you feel a whole lot better in a little while," she promised him, smiling impishly. "But first, you must tell me what happened to Pete Bergstrom."

Longarm sighed, filled the cup with more whiskey, and told her all of it. When he was finished, Annie shrugged.

"I don't see why you should feel so bad," she said. "He tried to kill you. And, for all you know, he would have if the Calico Kid hadn't shot him."

"I admit, it was damned uncomfortable heading back down that slope with Bergstrom's Sharps aimed at my back. But I don't think he would have shot me. I think he was satisfied by that time that I was who I said I was. The thing is, I came there to warn him—and, if possible, to save him from the Kid. I did neither. He knew all about the Calico Kid and, while he was dealing with me, the Kid cut him down." He shook his head and looked up at Annie with some exasperation. "Do you know what my score is now?"

"No," she said gently. "What is it, Longarm?"

"Zero. There are only six jurors left alive, and the Calico Kid is still out there aboard that bay of his, ready to cut down his next victim. I was not able to save Rawlings or Bergstrom, and Ned Koerner died trying to kill me."

She reached over and took his hand. "Don't feel so bad," she said. "Those jurors let a guilty man go free. The Calico Kid is only killing those who allowed a terrible miscarriage of justice. Maybe you shouldn't even be trying to save them."

"You don't really believe that, do you, Annie?"

Annie's casual comment surprised him. This was the first time she had spoken out so bluntly, and he was not pleased by her words. To hear a cold-blooded argument for vigilante behavior from such a fresh, warm-hearted young woman disappointed him.

"No," she said, looking quickly away from the disappointment in his eyes. "I suppose I don't, at that. It's just that I'd rather you stayed here with me instead of going off after the Kid." She looked back at him shyly. "You don't blame me for that, do you?"

He laughed. "I'd be a damned fool if I did," he said, finishing his drink and getting to his feet. "Come with me while I see to my horse for the night. Then maybe we can think of something else to do. How's that sound?"

"Delightful," Annie said.

They left the cabin together and, as Longarm led the chestnut over the barn, Annie's arm snaked around Longarm's slim waist. To the lawman, it felt just right.

The next morning, a few minutes after Longarm left for Lakewood City, Annie saddled a paint and headed across the lower meadow in back of the cabin. After traversing the meadow, she followed a stream into a thick stand of pine. A few moments later, her head down as she passed under a low branch, she heard the bay's whicker in the meadow ahead of her. Prince was cantering toward her when she broke from the timber.

She was pleased as always to see the horse—and doubly pleased that she had had the foresight to keep Prince here after her ride to Bergstrom's place. She intended to keep the bay out here from now on, and as a result had come out to spend some time with the powerful gelding. She felt bad about having left the horse out here for so long, but one look at its sleek flanks relieved her of any guilt. The bay was obviously enjoying its lazy time.

She only wished she could rid herself of the other

guilt she felt for continuing to deceive Longarm—a guilt that had been growing within her from the moment she realized how much she loved Deputy U. S. Marshal Custis Long.

Dismounting, she let the bay nuzzle her neck, then produced an apple. It vanished immediately, Prince's big lips nipping delicately over her palm. She talked to the horse for a while, patting its neck. She let the horse nudge her head gently, as it whickered softly all the while, asking for another apple.

She had come out to see how Prince was, but her mind kept returning to thoughts of Longarm. Longarm was on his way to warn a cattleman named Shoenburg, who lived just outside Lakewood City, and Annie had decided to let him do so. Longarm had been very upset by her opinion that perhaps the jurors deserved the fate being meted out to them. How disappointed—how horrified he would be if he ever found out that she was the Calico Kid.

But perhaps there was no need for him to find out— ever. As she had suggested to Longarm earlier, the Calico Kid could simply disappear.

Annie sighed deeply and hugged Prince's neck impulsively. Coming out here to visit Prince had given her the time she needed to think clearly. Glancing about her at the lovely parkland, she realized what she had—in this horse ranch of hers and in the love of a man like Longarm. She felt the weight of an enormous burden lift from her shoulders. She was suddenly very grateful that she was finished with the Calico Kid, and that Prince was no longer going to have to outdistance lead-throwing pursuers.

Annie patted Prince's head and sent him back to the meadow with a smart slap on his rump. She watched him for a while as he cantered off, then mounted the paint and rode back through the pines.

Something was wrong.

Annie couldn't tell what, exactly, but as she dismounted before her cabin, she could feel the hair rising on the back of her neck. She looked quickly about her but saw nothing unusual. The horses in the corral back of the second barn were quiet, and the few grazing in the upper meadow were in plain sight, their arching necks extended as they cropped the grass at their feet.

She left the paint and headed for the door. Before she reached it, the door was pulled open and Wes Hardy stepped into view. There was a terrible smile on his hateful face and in that instant she realized that, despite the decision she had just made to kill this man—the brutal murderer of her father—she would gladly become the Calico Kid once again.

Then Hardy stepped toward her. As he did so, he held something up in front of his face. Her calico scarf! He had found it!

With a furious scream, she rushed at him, her fingers hooked into claws. Standing his ground coolly, Wes stuffed the calico bandanna into his pocket, caught both her wrists in his powerful hands, and squeezed. The pain was excruciating, but Annie refused to utter a sound. When he finally let her go, she dropped to the ground, scalding tears of rage and pain streaming from her eyes. With a brutal chuckle, Wes reached down, grabbed Annie by the hair, and dragged her inside.

He did not let her go until he had deposited her on her bed. Then he methodically ripped her clothes from her and, despite her struggles, took her, coldly and without pleasure. When he was done with her she lay back, sobbing quietly, while he stood up and buttoned his britches.

"The Calico Kid," he said, musing. "Who'd ever believe it? I just laid the Calico Kid."

She looked up at him through eyes that smoked with hatred. "I hope you enjoyed it, you son of a bitch!"

He leaned over, smiled at her, then slapped her— hard. "I want a little more respect. I could have killed you when you rode in. And I would have been a hero if I had. That bay of yours and this calico scarf would have been all the proof I would have needed."

"You . . . know about Prince?"

"The bay gelding? Sure. I was on my way to Lakewood City when I camped in a meadow south of here. That's when I saw the bay, and old Reese's brand on its rump. I kept an eye out this morning, and when I saw you heading for the meadow, I circled back here to wait for you. While I waited, I looked around some and found your bandanna." He chuckled. "I knew Reese had a bastard child stashed somewhere, but I didn't know where. I don't think anyone else knew, though. That was something Reese spilled to me over a beer one night. He said you were in California. Said he was putting you through a fancy school." Hardy glanced with sniggering contempt at Annie's nakedness. "That must have been some school, honey."

"I am going to kill you."

"No, you won't. You'll be my secret love. And you won't ever let me down. Because if you do, I will have a story to tell. And when I do, you will hang, honey. Real high."

She leaped from the bed and flew at him. Snatching her wrists as he had before, he handled her just as casually and brutally. This time, however, he closed his hands about her wrists with such relentless pressure that they almost snapped. She was whimpering when he released her. Sagging to the floor, she rubbed her wrists anxiously, tears streaming down her cheeks.

"All right, bitch. Who was that rider I saw leaving here early this morning? He was too far away for me to ·get a line on him. But you sure as hell didn't sleep alone here last night."

Too quickly, Annie said. "No one you know."

Wes leaned close. "Now, how come you're so anxious to make me believe that?" He reached down and grabbed a handful of her hair, then twisted. "Who was it rode out this morning? Tell me, bitch, or you won't have no more hair."

"No!" she gasped.

With a brutal snap, Wes twisted his hand. Annie screamed. Again Wes twisted, and then lifted Annie off the floor.

"Longarm!" she screamed. "That U. S. deputy, Longarm!"

He flung her down and stepped back, frowning in happy concentration. "Longarm? Is that who that deputy is? I heard about him. This sure as hell is my lucky day. Yes, it purely is. Where was he headin' when he left here, bitch?"

"I don't know."

"I think you do."

As he started for her again, she pushed herself away from him until her back was against the wall. "I told you, I don't know where he was goin'!"

Wes reached down and pulled Annie to her feet. Then, holding her up with his left hand, he punched her in the jaw with his right. Annie lost consciousness. Wes waited. When her eyes flickered open, he punched her again. It took a little longer for Annie to regain her senses the second time.

When she did, Wes leaned close. "I can do this for most of the morning, bitch," he told her, grinning. "Where was that deputy going?"

Through her swollen mouth Annie mumbled, "Lakewood City."

"Who's he after there?"

"He's gone to warn Martin Shoenburg."

"That so?" he chuckled meanly. "Warn him against who? The Calico Kid?"

Wes let Annie go and stepped back to laugh. As swiftly as a cat, Annie darted past him, heading for the kitchen. She reached it ahead of him and snatched up a carving knife. Hard on her heels, Wes was too surprised to halt in time. Annie thrust deeply. Wes grunted, then staggered back, the carving knife's hilt sticking out of his side. He looked down in surprise at the knife protruding from him, and then at Annie.

"You cut me, you bitch!"

"No, you son of a bitch. I killed you."

"No, you didn't!" Wes snarled, pulling the knife out and flinging it away. "It hurts like hell, but I ain't dead yet."

Annie darted past him and out the door. As she ran across the yard, she screamed back at him, "You'll be dead soon enough!"

With an angry snarl, Wes took after her. Ignoring the painful wound, he overtook Annie in front of the nearest barn and, with one powerful swipe, knocked her to the ground. Then he began kicking her. Annie twisted into a ball and hugged herself as he flailed away. At last, exhausted by his insane, ungovernable fury, Wes staggered and went down on one knee.

Annie slowly uncoiled and looked over at him. She could hardly move, she was so sore. Every breath she took caused a tearing, gasping pain to erupt in her right side. Wes was looking down at the wound in his side. His trouser leg was slick with blood clear down to his boot.

"Bitch," he rasped, and limped painfully into the barn.

A moment later he rode out, guiding his mount directly at her. At the last moment, Annie managed to roll out of the way. Wes kept on, glancing back, at her.

"I'll be back, bitch!" he called. "Keep that bed warm!"

Annie sagged to the ground, sobbing. The earth tipped alarmingly under her, and before she could help herself, she rolled off the edge into darkness.

Arriving in Lakewood City later that same day, Longarm dismounted in front of the town's only saloon and went inside to wet his whistle.

Sipping his second cold beer, he learned from the barkeep that Shoenburg called his ranch the Bar S. It was no more than a two-hour ride from Lakewood City. According to the barkeep, it was not much more than three, or at the most four quarter sections, boasting poor grass and a scarcity of water, tied together with barbed wire. Shoenburg was trying to run the operation without a wife, and with his nineteen-year-old daughter serving as his only hand.

Thanking the barkeep, Longarm left the saloon and started for Shoenburg's ranch. It was close on to sunset when the lawman topped a sandy ridge and saw the sun-bleached buildings that comprised the Bar S.

As he angled down the ridge, he caught sight of a rider approaching from the west. He pulled up and waited. Not until the rider was almost upon him did he realize that it was a girl. Shoenburg's daughter, Longarm surmised at once.

She wore Levi's, a red-checked cotton shirt, a red bandanna, and a black, flat-crowned Stetson. She forked the big gelding she rode as well as any man.

"Where you headin', mister?" she asked Longarm as she pulled her mount to a halt in front of him.

"The Bar S."

"You found it. What can I do for you?"

"Are you Martin Shoenburg's daughter?"

"I am."

"Pleased to meet you," Longarm said, touching his hat brim. "I am Custis Long, a deputy U.S. marshal. I'm here to see your father."

"Do you have a badge, Marshal?"

Longarm pulled out his wallet and handed it to her. She took it from him, flipped it open, and glanced at the shield. Handing his wallet back to him, she said, "I'm Ellen Shoenburg. Is this about the Calico Kid?"

"It is. I came out here to warn your father—and to help, if I can."

"We know all about the Kid, Marshal."

"It has been a long ride," Longarm told her gently, smiling as he spoke. "You don't suppose there might be a fresh pot of coffee somewhere nearby?"

She smiled slightly, and he saw at once how pretty she could be when she was not acting as her father's ramrod. "Of course, Marshal. I'm sure Father must have some fresh coffee on the stove. You are welcome to ride in and set a spell."

"Thank you."

As they rode toward the ranch buildings, Longarm could not help but notice how coolly Ellen Shoenburg was taking not only Longarm's visit, but the threat represented by the Calico Kid. The only thing he could figure was that her apparent lack of emotion was simply a way of controlling the genuine fear she must feel. She was a slim, intelligent-looking girl with dark eyes and shimmering, shoulder-length hair almost as black as an Indian's.

Riding close beside her, he said, "Your father understands, does he, why the Calico Kid is after him?"

"Yes, Marshal. He understands only too well."

"Do you mind, Ellen, if I ask if you understand?"

"What do you mean?"

"Why did your father vote for acquittal? Surely he knew Wes Hardy was guilty."

Without blinking, Ellen said, "Look around you, Marshal, at this sorry excuse for a cattle ranch. My father was desperate. When Wes Hardy offered him money to dig his heels in for an acquittal, my father did not hesitate."

"You don't think there was anything wrong in that?"

She glanced at him and he felt her sudden, icy contempt. "What are you trying to get me to say, Marshal? That I think my father was a fool to let himself be bribed?"

"I just wanted to know how you felt about it."

"I hate it, Marshal. And so does my father. He has other troubles to contend with, and now, with the news of what happened to those other two jurors in Mills Falls, he has become quite despondent."

Longarm almost pulled his mount to a halt. "What was that about two men in Mills Falls?"

"You mean you weren't aware of what happened to them?"

Longarm mentally scanned the list of jurors Billy Vail had given him. There were two members of the jury,

92

business partners in Mills Falls, whom he had not contacted yet. "Are you referring to Jim Tillson and Cal Rivkin?" he asked.

She nodded briskly. "Yes, I am."

Longarm sighed. He felt more than a little useless all of a sudden. "I guess I am having some difficulty keeping up with the Calico Kid," he told her ruefully. "Perhaps you could fill me in."

By that time, they had reached the yard in front of the main cabin. The yard was not well kept and much of the fencing was in need of repair. An air of poverty and neglect hung over the place. As Longarm pulled up, he noticed that the front door hung open slightly.

"Later, Marshal," Ellen told Longarm as she dismounted and started ahead of him toward the cabin. "After supper, perhaps."

She seemed suddenly apprehensive. Perhaps her father wasn't all that good a cook, Longarm thought wryly.

"I'll see to the horses," he told her, dismounting.

"Thank you," she called, pushing the door all the way open and entering the cabin.

Leading both horses, Longarm had almost reached the barn when he heard Ellen's scream. It caused a cold chill to run up his back. Dropping both sets of reins, he drew his Colt and raced for the cabin.

Ellen Shoenburg was still screaming when he bolted into the cabin. She was facing a half-open bedroom door, her head down, her eyes shielded by both hands. Looking beyond her, Longarm caught a glimpse of a human form hanging from the ceiling of the darkened bedroom.

Once again, he was too late. Martin Shoenburg had hanged himself.

* * *

It was dark when Longarm rode back into Lakewood City, Ellen Shoenburg riding at his side, the dead rancher wrapped in a blanket and slung over the saddle of the horse Longarm was leading. After seeing to a room for himself and one for the girl at the Lakewood City Hotel, Longarm went looking for an undertaker. That sad business completed, he left the horses at the town's livery stable and returned to the hotel.

A small crowd had gathered by this time, most of the curious citizens clustering on the hotel porch. Pushing himself through the crowd, Longarm declined to reply to any of their questions as he moved on into the hotel and mounted the narrow stairs to Ellen's room.

He knocked gently. Ellen opened the door and let him in.

"You're going to have to deal with some very curious citizens," he told her, taking off his hat and sitting on the edge of the bed.

"No, I won't," Ellen told him softly but firmly. "They don't have to know anything more than they do now: that Dad is dead."

"I am afraid the undertaker will know precisely what happened. And he's liable to blab."

"Let him. That's his privilege. But they'll learn nothing from me."

"Or me."

"Thank you, Longarm."

Longarm looked at her. Back in the cabin she had stopped screaming the moment he placed both hands gently on her shoulders. There had been no need for him to shake her or even to comfort her. With remarkable control, she had stepped ahead of him into the bedroom and glanced up at the grotesquely frozen body of her father. Reaching out, she touched his boot lightly, softly bade him goodbye, then turned and retreated to her own bedroom.

To say that Longarm was impressed by the girl's iron composure was putting it mildly. The problem was that he expected at any moment to see her crack, and when that happened, he wondered if he would be able to pick up the pieces.

She seemed to have read his mind. "You're worried about me, aren't you, Longarm?"

"Yes," he admitted, "I am."

"You don't have to be. I will be all right. Dad was a sick man, too sick to work the ranch. And he was in great pain. I don't know what it was. But he knew he wasn't going to get any better, and he refused to see a doctor. This Calico Kid business was the final straw. I think I know what he was thinking when he placed that noose around his neck. He was attempting to simplify matters for all of us."

"Simplify matters?"

"He was like that, Longarm. He hated complications. His illness and that miserable trial were complications enough. And now the Calico Kid. He definitely did not want to have to deal with that, as well."

"So he decided to simplify matters for the Calico Kid."

"And for me."

"I am glad you can handle this so calmly."

She did not reply.

Longarm stood up and cleared his throat. "You told me earlier that two more jurors had been killed by the Calico Kid. What can you tell me about that, Ellen?"

Coldly, without embellishment, she told Longarm how the two men had disappeared from their place of business and how later that same night, the Calico Kid had ridden down Mills Falls' main street, dragging their two bodies behind him.

Longarm hid his bitter sense of defeat as best he could, thanked her, and put his hat back on. "You sure you're going to be all right now?" he asked as he pulled the door open.

"Yes, Longarm," she told him. "My mother's people live in Denver City. As soon as I sell the Bar S, I'll be moving there. Thank you for your concern."

Marveling once again at her composure, Longarm nodded goodbye and pulled the door shut behind him. Before starting off down the hallway, however, he paused, resting his head lightly against the door's panel. What he heard saddened him, but relieved him of his concern for Ellen.

In the solitude of her hotel room, Ellen was crying softly, letting the grief she felt finally express itself. She was not an unfeeling woman of stone, after all. She was as human as anyone else. The only difference was her impressive self-control—and her courage.

Considerably sobered, Longarm moved off down the hallway, looking forward to a drink at the saloon across the street. And just possibly he would find the time for more than one drink while he was at it. This unsettling news about Jim Tillson and Cal Rivkin was as good a reason as any.

Still weak from Annie's knife wound, Wes Hardy leaned against the wall beside the window of his hotel room and watched the big lawman shoulder his way past the saloon's bat wings.

As Longarm disappeared from sight, Hardy sat carefully down onto his bed and leaned back gingerly. Annie's knife had not sliced into any vital organs, and a local sawbones had already sewed up the wound, but the pain was constant and nagging. And he was still somewhat lightheaded from loss of blood. Nevertheless, as he settled cautiously back onto his pillow, there was a smile on his face. He had found Longarm, and when that big son of a bitch left Lakewood City, Wes was confident he would have no difficulty following him.

What Wes had to consider now was how he would kill Longarm when the time came. A bizarre but intriguing plan was already insinuating itself into his thoughts, and the more he considered it, the greater was his enthusiasm. As sure as bears shit in the woods, he was going to take care of Longarm, and then it would be Howie Murphy's turn. But the sweetest part of it all was that both killings would leave him free and clear of any suspicion. He was going to let the Calico Kid take all the credit.

Exulting in this thought, Wes Hardy closed his eyes to stop the room's dark walls from spinning about him, and fell into a deep, healing sleep.

Chapter 7

As Wes Hardy slept, Longarm returned to the hotel an hour or so later and knocked gently on Ellen's door. Ellen let him into her room, grateful that he had come to see her.

"I'm moving out soon," Longarm told her. "I'm trying to keep ahead of the Calico Kid. But I didn't want to leave without checking to see how you were."

"That was very kind of you."

"How do you feel, Ellen?"

"How do I feel?" She laughed shortly, bitterly. "Empty, Longarm. Empty and bitter."

"I'm sorry."

She shook her head wearily. "Everything Dad tried went sour on him. That miserable, unproductive ranch. Then his illness. And then that awful jury duty." She peered unhappily up at him. "You must understand, Longarm. He was so sick. All he wanted was to get away

99

from that stifling courthouse, to come back to me and the ranch. The money was important, too, but it wasn't the entire reason. You must see that!"

He reached out and took hold of her shoulders. "It's all right, Ellen. You don't have to say any more. I understand."

She twisted her head away so he would not see her tears. Her shoulders began to tremble. Stepping closer, he put both arms around her and held her gently.

In a while, her quiet, pitiable weeping ceased, and he led her over to her bed. When he tried to pull away, however, she flung her arms around him and drew him still closer to her with the urgency of a small child. He did not argue with her need and lay on the bed beside her, holding her tightly, allowing her to cling to him. Not until she was finally asleep did he carefully disengage himself, stand up, and quietly go to his own room for a few hours' rest.

Not long after Longarm rode out of Lakewood City, heading for Cottonwood. The moon was a bleary red eye hanging in the night sky. Aside from Howard Murphy, there were just two jurors left. Longarm didn't give a damn about Murphy, but he was damned if he was going to let the Calico Kid get the other two.

John Hightower, Longarm had already established from some men in the saloon in Lakewood City, was a sodbuster who owned a small farm just outside Cottonwood. Asa Fuller was a gambler who lived in Cottonwood. The Gold Nugget was the saloon he favored. When Longarm rode into Cottonwood just after dawn the next day, the town was already waking up, but the Gold Nugget was as silent as the grave.

Dismounting in front of a small restaurant, Longarm

entered and did his best to fill the yawning cavern beneath his ribs. Sipping his coffee, he asked the buxom waitress if she knew where he could find the living quarters of Asa Fuller.

The gambler lived over the saloon across the street. Longarm paid up and crossed the street to the two-story frame building that housed the saloon. Outside wooden steps led to the second floor. Longarm mounted them and knocked on the door. He got no response after his first knock or his second.

He was about to use the butt of his .44 when the door was abruptly yanked open and Longarm found himself staring into the muzzles of two gleaming, pearl-handled Colts. The owner of all this firepower was a grim shadow of a man almost as tall as Longarm, with a face that looked as if it had been carved out of ivory with a jack-knife. His gleaming black eyes were hidden deep within shadowed sockets. On his head the man wore a black Stetson, but aside from that, he was naked.

"Asa Fuller?" Longarm inquired pleasantly enough.

"Who the hell are you?"

"Deputy U. S. Marshal Custis Long. And I am pleased indeed to see that you are alive, Mr. Fuller. But it looks to me like you might end up catching pneumonia if you ain't careful."

Frowning, Asa glanced down at his nakedness, then back at Longarm. "You come about that crazy rider, the Calico Kid?"

Longarm nodded.

"I don't need your help, Marshal."

"But maybe I need yours."

"I'm tired. Just got to bed. Come back later."

"Sleep later. Right now I want to talk."

Asa looked into Longarm's grim, determined eyes and

shrugged. Stepping back, he held the door open as the lawman walked into his small, cluttered room. Once inside, Longarm waited while Asa returned his two bright weapons to the gunbelt slung over his bedpost. Then he pulled on a pair of slick, faun-colored britches and sat down on his bed. So light a burden was he that the bed hardly sagged under him.

"All right," Asa said, "talk."

"I figure the Calico Kid will be looking for you soon. He's about run out of jurors. So I'm proposing that you ride out to John Hightower's place with me. Together, the three of us should be a match for the Calico Kid."

"You mean wait for him out there?"

"That's right."

"Might be a long wait."

Longarm shrugged. "So far, the Calico Kid hasn't wasted much time. I suggest it is the safest course for you and Hightower to follow—if you want to stay alive, that is."

"I want to live, Marshal. But I keep my own body-guards real close. In those two holsters over there."

"They're pretty enough, I'll admit. But they don't fire by themselves, and they sleep when you do."

Sighing, Asa nodded. "When do you want to set out for Hightower's place?"

"Now."

Asa shook his head unhappily. "Guess I should have figured this. I held some pretty miserable cards last night, and the filly I was supposed to bed with skipped out with another gent. Like they say, it never rains but it pours." He smiled coldly at Longarm. "Give me half an hour. I'll get my gear ready and meet you downstairs at the livery."

"I'll be waiting," Longarm said.

As soon as Wes Hardy awoke that morning, he hurried downstairs to be ready to follow Longarm out of town. Watching from the livery stable, he saw the Shoenburg girl leave the hotel, cross the dusty street, and enter the undertaker's place alone. Anxiously, Wes waited to see if Longarm would join her. When he didn't, Wes hurried across the street to the hotel and asked the desk clerk if his good friend Deputy U.S. Marshal Long was still registered.

Anxious to placate the big man with the hard eyes, the clerk consulted his register and told Wes that Long had already checked out.

"When, dammit?" Wes growled.

"I don't know," the clerk answered, glancing quickly down at the register. "But it must have been before I came on this morning."

"Sometime last night, then."

"Yes, sir."

With a silent curse, Wes turned and hurried up to his room. He had a pretty good idea where the lawman had gone. Two of the jurors lived near Cottonwood. As he hurriedly packed his gear, he muttered unhappily. He had not expected to have to move this fast.

"Just look at that, will you," said Asa, as he stood in his stirrups to peer at the Hightower farm. "What a miserable spread. And the human pigs grunting in this particular sty are probably happy."

Longarm did not reply. But he could not deny that his own feelings closely matched the gambler's. Though Hightower's place was not as dilapidated as Pete Bergstrom's, it was almost as bad. The front yard was littered with broken carriages and rotting bits of harness. A broken wash bucket had been turned over and a Rhode Island Red was perched on it, surveying the devastation. The powerful smell wafting from the pigpen had reached them long before their horses entered the farm compound. One barn had already lost a portion of its roof, and the outhouse looked about ready to topple over as it sat precariously on a rocky tuft of ground beside the cabin.

Crowded in the doorway were Hightower, his wife, a daughter who looked close to eighteen, and four smaller youngsters, two girls and two boys. The older daughter had long hair the color of corn silk and large blue eyes. The skimpy dress she wore did little to hide her high-breasted, burgeoning ripeness. Hightower's wife had a slack expression and graying hair pulled severely back into a bun, and was wearing a shapeless sack dress. The four youngsters ranged in age from three to seven. The two youngest were barefoot and the smallest, a boy, was naked below the waist.

As Longarm and Asa pulled up before the cabin, another kid, a towheaded boy of ten or eleven, came charging around the corner of the cabin at full gallop. He halted when he saw the two riders, then bolted for the cabin doorway.

Shucking his hat back off his forehead, Longarm called, "Howdy. My name's Long. Custis Long. We've come out here to see what we can do to help."

The lanky Hightower left the doorway and started carefully across the yard toward them. He was carrying an ancient but well-kept Kentucky rifle. Pausing in front of their horses, he squinted up at them. "What's that you say? What for did you come out here?"

"To help you."

"Why?"

"The Calico Kid."

"The who?"

"Ain't you heard about the Calico Kid, Hightower?" Asa asked.

"Nope."

"Well, you should have," Longarm drawled.

"Why?"

"Because the Calico Kid has already killed a lot of the jurors that set Wes Hardy free."

Hightower frowned, then looked from one to the other. "Hadn't heard," he said. "Been pretty busy."

Glancing quickly around, Longarm wondered what the man had been busy doing. Then he saw the herd of young 'uns.

"Well, that don't matter," Longarm persisted. "We've come out here to set a trap for the Kid, and we'd like your cooperation."

Hightower grew alert. His eyes narrowed. "How much?"

"How much what?"

Hightower sent a long stream of tobacco juice at a small clump of grass at his feet. "How much you payin' me to cooperate?"

"Why, hell, man," Asa exploded, "we're here to save your life. And you want us to pay you?"

"We goin' to have to feed you?"

"Maybe," said Asa truculently.

"Where you two goin' to sleep?" the farmer continued.

"The barn would do nicely," Longarm said quickly.

"Can't."

"Why not, dammit?" Asa was getting riled.

"My young 'uns sleep in there. And we don't have much food. Ain't been a good year for us."

105

Longarm looked at Asa. He was stumped. He had ridden hard, recruited Asa Fuller, and come out here to save a man he had imagined was waiting with quaking fear for the arrival of a Nemesis that had already accounted for the lives of six of his fellow jurors. And Hightower couldn't care less.

"You got any coffee?" Longarm asked, exasperated.

"Nope. We're real short, Long."

"We'll camp close by for now," Longarm said, sighing. "I assume it will be all right if we use your well."

"Ain't no way to get the water out. Windmill's broke." The man's rheumy eyes lit up momentarily. "Maybe you could fix it."

"We'll find a stream," Longarm said shortly, pulling his horse around.

It was dark when a weary Wes Hardy reached the Hightower farm. He had found out what he needed to know in Cottonwood. Longarm and the gambler had ridden out earlier that morning, heading for the Hightower place. It was clear what they intended. They were setting a trap for the Calico Kid, and Longarm was probably holed up in the house now, waiting.

Reining in just outside the farm compound, Wes carefully dismounted. He was not moving freely. The wound in his side had been acting up for the last three or four hours. Twice he had been forced to dismount to give himself a rest.

He peered toward the darkened cabin. There was no light coming from it. The sound of crickets was deafening. He glanced toward the barn, frowning. He would hit that first, he figured. The thing was, how could he be certain that Longarm was staked out inside the house?

He could be anywhere around here. Glancing swiftly around him, he guided his horse around toward the rear of the barn.

He was almost abreast of it when he heard laughter and the sound of sudden movement coming from the place. Pulling up, he froze. He heard it again. Kids! There were kids in the barn, raising hell even though they should have been asleep. Wes grinned. Hightower's family was inside the barn, hiding out. Longarm was inside the cabin, waiting.

A neat trap. Only Wes Hardy had already cottoned to it.

Reaching into his pocket, Wes took out the calico bandanna and tied it around his neck. Then he led his horse into a dark copse nearby. Selecting two dead branches that were lying about in the timber, he tied some torn pieces of an old cotton shirt of his about them, climbed back onto his horse, lit the cotton, and rode from the copse, both torches blazing. As he neared the farmyard, he pulled the calico bandanna up over his face.

His plan was simplicity itself. He would fire the barn, drawing Longarm out of the cabin. Then he would cut the lawman down—and Hightower too, if he showed his face. Riding off, he would be identified as the Calico Kid. And there would be one more reason why Annie Reese would have to settle down and enjoy his company.

He flung one torch up onto the barn's roof. To his surprise, it disappeared almost immediately through a hole. A chorus of screams erupted from the barn. Pleased, Wes flung his other torch at the barn's entrance. Immediately it flared up as the flames fed on the loose hay. A garish, flickering light flooded the compound.

Wes turned his rifle on the cabin doorway just as the

door was flung open. A tall, unmistakable figure loomed in the doorway, a rifle in his hand. Wes fired, and was sure that the lawman crumpled. But even as he went down, he managed to get off a shot. The bullet slammed into Wes's shoulder.

"Damn!" Wes cried as the force of the round almost knocked him from his saddle. Tugging cruelly on his reins, he wheeled his horse and galloped back across the farmyard, heading for the distant hills.

As he rode, he had only one consolation. He had cut down Longarm. Now it was Murphy's turn.

When Longarm saw Wes's first torch flare into life, he awakened Asa and started for his horse. By the time Wes had lit the second torch and ridden into the farmyard, both men were galloping down the slope toward Hightower's place. The short, sudden exchange of gunfire occurred well before Longarm and Asa reached the farm, however, and as Longarm rode up, he saw the Calico Kid disappearing toward the hills.

For a moment Longarm was tempted to go after him, but by then the barn was exploding into flames. Hightower's wife, screaming at the top of her lungs, was rushing toward the blazing building, her husband—limping painfully—right on her heels. Never had Longarm felt so much frustration. But there was no doubt in his mind which way he should go.

Cutting into the farmyard, he and Asa reached the barn a few minutes after Hightower and his wife did. Plunging in after them, they helped lead the Hightowers' two frantic work horses from the barn, while John and his wife pushed and cuffed their children through a gaping hole in the rear of the barn.

Once the work horses and the children were safely

outside, the family turned their attention to Hightower. He had been wounded in the earlier exchange with the Calico Kid, but only now had he allowed himself to admit it.

Slumped on the ground in front of his cabin while his wife yanked down his Levi's to tend to a messy-looking thigh wound, he looked up at Longarm. "You two must've been real close."

"We were on the ridge."

Hightower grunted. "You was in the same county, sure enough."

The blazing barn lit the farmyard as bright as day. In its garish light, Longarm watched as the eighteen-year-old blonde hurried to her father's side with a pan of water. A much younger daughter appeared with a pair of scissors and fresh sheets.

As Hightower's woman began cutting through the sheets to make bandages, Longarm glanced nervously at Asa. The reason the two of them had camped on that ridge so far away was the stench coming from the Hightowers' pigpen. It had seemed to follow them and had kept them moving their camp farther and farther away until at last they had found themselves on the ridge. But both men were loath to admit this to the Hightowers.

"Is there anything we can do?" Longarm asked lamely.

Hightower glanced at the barn. It was collapsing in on itself now, pumping sparks and blazing cinders into the night sky.

"Nope," he said.

Leaning close to get a better view, Asa said, "You ain't hurt too bad, looks like."

"Bad enough."

"That's so, of course," Asa admitted.

"Sounded like the Kid fired twice," said Longarm.

"Nope. He fired once."

"You mean you got off a shot?"

"Yup." Hightower grimaced slightly as his wife began scrubbing at his wound.

"Pa hit him," the woman said, glancing up from her husband's torn thigh.

"You sure of that?" Longarm asked, immediately alert.

"She just told you so, didn't she?" Hightower snapped.

"How badly was he hurt?"

"Almost knocked him off his horse."

"It was the Calico Kid for sure?" Asa asked.

"I don't know the son of a bitch, so how would I know for sure it was him? I was busy gettin' shot at. Besides, he had a bandanna over his face."

"It was the Calico Kid, all right," Asa said.

"The horse he rode?" Longarm asked Hightower. "Was it a bay?"

"Nope."

"What was it?"

"Beats the shit out of me. A roan, maybe."

Longarm looked at Asa. "I'm going after him. If he's wounded and no longer riding that bay, I might have a chance to overtake him. Stay here and look after the Hightowers."

Asa nodded quickly, his eyes on the tall blonde. "I'll be glad to do that, Longarm," he said.

"We don't need no help," protested Hightower.

"Yes, we do, Pa," the oldest daughter said. "Now you hush and let the man stay if he wants." She glanced at Asa and smiled.

"You heard her, Pa," said Hightower's wife. "You listen to Anna May and set still while I finish with this here wound. You're bleedin' like a stuck pig!"

Grumbling, Hightower offered no more resistance to

the idea. As Longarm mounted up, he saw a pleased grin on Asa's face. At that moment it occurred to Longarm that something pleasant might come out of this night's unpleasantness after all.

Wheeling his horse, he rode off in the direction the Calico Kid had taken.

Chapter 8

It took Annie some time to recover, not only from the beating, but from the knowledge that she had told Wes Hardy where to find Longarm. A day after Wes left her unconscious in the dust of her front yard, she gathered her gear together, mounted her bay, and took off after him.

She reached Lakewood City too late to catch Wes Hardy, and when she rode into Martin Shoenburg's spread, she found no one there. There was a desolation about the place that chilled her. She did not stay long.

Returning to Lakewood City, she found it difficult to ask questions about either Wes Hardy or Longarm. She could not just walk into the saloon and make inquiries. Her presence in such places, as she knew from bitter experience, raised too many eyebrows and brought her an unwelcome abundance of propositions.

She took her inquiries to the livery instead. There, while currying Prince, she struck up a conversation with the grizzled old hostler in charge. It did not take long for her to learn about the arrival of a tall lawman and the death by hanging of Martin Shoenburg soon thereafter. The lawman had ridden out in the direction of Cottonwood before dawn two days before, with a man that fit Wes Hardy's description riding out after him later that same morning.

Annie knew the names and the approximate addresses of each jury member. John Hightower ran a small farm just outside Cottonwood, and there was a gambler, Asa Fuller, who frequented a saloon in Cottonwood. She fed her bay, watered it, and rode out of Lakewood City, arriving in Cottonwood close to sundown the next day. She checked into the hotel to plan her next move and to rest. She was still a very sore young lady.

Wes Hardy had intended to cut for Murphy's spread, but his wound gave him more trouble than he had expected it would. Nevertheless, buoyed by the conviction that he had killed Longarm, he refused to be dismayed. He dug a deerskin jacket out of his bedroll to cover his shoulder wound and headed back for Cottonwood to find another sawbones.

It was still dark when he reached Cottonwood. Pulling up beside a parson leaving town in a buggy, he was directed to a doctor who lived in a small white frame house on the outskirts of the town. Pulling up before the house, Wes slid off his roan and walked up the narrow walk leading to the porch. To his surprise, the three porch steps gave him some trouble, but he shook off the mo-

114

mentary dizziness and knocked solidly on the door. He had to knock more than once before the doctor pulled the door open.

The doctor was at least a foot shorter than Wes and was wearing spectacles. A napkin was tucked under his high collar, indicating that he had been interrupted at his supper.

"The office is closed," the doctor said. "Come back tomorrow at nine—unless it's an emergency."

With a gentleness that surprised himself, Wes said, "I guess maybe it *is* an emergency, Doc. I caught a round in my shoulder. I'd like you to dig it out and stop the bleeding."

"My God," the doc muttered. "Come in. Come in!" He closed the door behind Wes and led him swiftly into his small office.

Wes sat on a stool beside the operating table and let the doctor cut away the shirt from around the slug's point of entry. The doctor stepped back in surprise when he pulled off Wes's shirt. The numerous scars and recently acquired wounds that covered Wes's powerful torso, especially the welts left by Howard Murphy's bullwhip, obviously stunned the physician.

"Looks to me," muttered the doctor, "like you've been through a deal of trouble—and some of it lately."

"Never mind that, Doc. Can you get that slug out?"

"Yes," the doctor said, peering closely at the torn shoulder. "But I'll have to dig some." He looked with some concern at Wes. "I have some chloroform. Do you want me to use it?"

"It'll put me out, right, Doc?"

"It has that remarkable property, yes. It might make you act a little silly, as well. But you won't feel a thing when I probe for the bullet."

"Never mind using that stuff, Doc. Just go in there and dig it out."

The doctor's eyebrows shot up a notch. "As you wish."

Patiently, Wes stared up at a corner of the ceiling as the doctor took up his forceps and began to dig. Beads of sweat were standing out on Wes's forehead a full minute later when the doctor finally withdrew the slug. As relieved as Wes Hardy, the doctor showed his patient the round.

Wes glanced at it casually, then looked again. "Let me see that," he growled, his face suddenly darkening.

The doctor handed it to him. Grabbing it in his right hand, Wes examined it, his fury and disappointment growing.

"Damn!" Wes exploded. "This here round didn't come from no Colt, nor no Winchester, neither!"

"Let me see that," said the doctor. Examining it, he said, "I've fished for quite a few of these back in the hills. A Kentucky rifle sent this round, I'm thinking. A Hawken, maybe."

Wes snatched the flattened round back, glanced down once more at it, then flung it into a corner. "Hurry up, Doc. Get me out of here. I got unfinished business."

Reaching for a whiskey bottle, the doctor nodded. "Hang on," he told Wes. "This is going to sting some."

Wes closed his eyes and grimaced as the doc poured the whiskey into the raw hole in Wes's shoulder. Then, swiftly, he packed the wound and wound a tight bandage about the shoulder.

Finished, he stepped back and said, "Let me fix a sling for that left arm of yours."

"Never mind that," said Wes, standing up and thrusting his left hand in between the buttons of his buckskin jacket. "How much do I owe you?"

The doc shrugged. "Two dollars."

"Here's a silver dollar," Wes said, digging into his back pocket with his right hand and flipping the coin at the man. "I'll pay you the rest next time I see you."

The doctor did not argue as he pocketed the coin, which was a good thing. As Wes Hardy stomped out of the small frame house, his anger and disappointment were mounting considerably. Climbing carefully back onto his horse, he continued on into Cottonwood, left his horse at the livery stable, then crossed to the saloon.

By his second beer, he had calmed down somewhat. Longarm had been out there at that sodbuster's farm, waiting for the Calico Kid. Of that Wes was almost certain. And, as far as that big lawman knew, it was the Calico Kid who had struck at Hightower's place—not Wes Hardy.

That meant Wes could calm down and relax and wait for his next shot at the big son of a bitch. Which wouldn't take long; not if the lawman could read sign. Like as not, he was on his way to Cottonwood right now, looking for the Calico Kid.

Feeling somewhat better, though a little woozy from loss of blood, Hardy flagged the barkeep. He wanted another beer.

Longarm was able to use the light from the burning barn to pick up and follow the Calico Kid's trail, and when he had left the glow far behind him, the moon helped some. But before long the night had defeated him and he lost all sign of the Calico Kid's trail.

By that time, however, he was heading in a straight line for Cottonwood, so he kept on riding. When he reached the town, he left his horse at the livery stable and asked the hostler if there was a doctor nearby. He then set out for the small white frame house on the edge of town where Dr. Tom Witherspoon lived and had his office. A small, weary man wearing steel-rimmed spectacles answered Longarm's knock.

"Dr. Witherspoon?" Longarm asked.

"That's me. If what ails you is not an emergency, I suggest you come back tomorrow at nine."

"There's nothing that ails me, Doc," Longarm replied. "I'm a law officer, a deputy U. S. marshal, and I am looking for a man supposed to be wounded. I was hoping you could help me."

With a sigh, the doctor said, "Come in, Marshal. You can ask your questions while I wash my instruments."

A moment later, leaning against the doorjamb in the office, Longarm listened to the doctor describe the operation he had just performed and the individual for whom he had performed it. Finishing up his account, the doc looked up at Longarm, his mild gray eyes wide behind his spectacles. "You should have seen his chest and back. That man has been through some fierce encounters. I saw the marks of whip lashes, a knife wound and at least one other gunshot wound."

"But you figure he was big enough to handle all that damage."

"It certainly seemed so."

"That round you took out of him—you got it?"

The doctor nodded and took the washed and polished slug out of a glass dish on one of his counters. "He seemed quite upset when I showed it to him. He had expected a .44-40, something from a Colt or a Winchester, I believe."

Longarm inspected the flattened round for a second or two, then handed it back to the doctor. "A Kentucky rifle shot this round," he said.

The little man smiled. "That's what I told my visitor."

"Which way did he go when he left here?"

"On into town. My guess is he went somewhere to tickle his tonsils. He'd be needing a lift about now, I'm thinking."

"Yes, he would."

Longarm thanked the doctor, clapped his hat back on, and left the small house. Mounting up, he rode into Cottonwood, his brow furrowed as he tried to piece this lunatic puzzle together.

From all the evidence, it appeared that the man Hightower had shot—the Calico Kid—had just been treated by Dr. Witherspoon. The problem was that Witherspoons' description of the Calico Kid did not match Longarm's knowledge of what the Kid was supposed to look like.

The doctor had described a man at least six feet four or five inches tall, red-haired, with massive shoulders and powerful, rippling muscles.

In other words, Wes Hardy.

On the other hand, witnesses who had seen the Calico Kid had always described him as a slight, youthful man who rode as light as a jockey. There was no way those two descriptions could be reconciled. Wes Hardy and the Calico Kid were two different people.

But that didn't mean that Wes Hardy could not have dug up a calico scarf for himself and ridden out to the Hightower place in an attempt to kill Hightower.

The only question that remained was why? Why on earth should Hardy want to kill one of the jurors who was instrumental in setting him free?

With a baleful stare, Wes Hardy watched the nervous barkeep approaching his table. Wes was the last patron in the saloon, and for some time now it had been obvious to him that the barkeep was anxious to close up. Well, goddammit, Wes was not ready to go yet. And if this little shit tried to put him out, he would part his hair with the stein he was holding.

"Ain't that nice—you coming over to my table," Wes said, wincing slightly as he moved his shoulder forward. "I'd like another beer."

"I'd like to close up now, mister," the barkeep said.

"You would, would you?"

"It's late."

"I don't give a damn how late it is. Get me another beer."

The little man went white. He reacted to Wes's words as if he had been slapped. Pulling up, he swallowed unhappily. "You . . . want another beer?"

"You heard me!"

The barkeep turned and hurried back to the bar. A grin on his big face, Wes watched the barkeep draw the beer, then skim off its head with a straight edge. Mopping his brow nervously, the little fellow set the beer down on the counter, then reached under it to come up with a sawed-off shotgun.

With a curse, Wes scrambled to his feet, lifting his Colt from its holster and aiming at the barkeep in one furious move. As the chair went over behind him, he fired. It was a lucky shot. He caught the barkeep in the face and sent him reeling into his shelf of whiskey bottles. The shotgun detonated, punching a ragged hole in the ceiling over Wes's head.

The sudden movement had caused a sharp dagger of pain to radiate out from his shoulder, but Wes Hardy took a grim satisfaction in the fact that his shot had been so successful. Still, he would have preferred the beer.

He strode over to the bar, grabbed the stein, and, ignoring the dead man slumped crookedly behind the bar, drained it. Then he holstered his weapon and started for the bat wings.

As he pushed his way through them and paused on the saloon porch, he saw that at this late hour the gunfire had drawn only two curious men, both of whom were watching him now from across the street. Cottonwood had no local constable, Wes knew, so he did not expect any trouble as he stared coldly across the street at the two men. But he did not forget that Longarm might be reaching Cottonwood soon, and he glanced up and down the dark street for any sign of the lawman. When he saw none, he turned his attention back to the two men standing on the sidewalk across from the saloon.

"That stupid little barkeep in there tried to blast me," Wes told them. "You better get someone to plant the son of a bitch."

"Who the hell are you?" one of the men asked nervously.

"Never mind. Just get that stupid barkeep out of there before he stinks up the place."

One of the men hurried off. Moving carefully to keep down the throbbing in his shoulder, Wes started down the steps on his way to the hotel. He was just about ready to call it a night.

Longarm had also heard the explosion of gunfire from the saloon. He had been stabling his black at the time. Moving swiftly to the livery doorway, he kept within the shadows and watched the saloon. When Wes Hardy strode defiantly out onto the porch, Longarm shook his head and grunted softly.

The moment he heard those shots, he should have

known it was Wes Hardy. The big redhead had a remarkable gift for getting and keeping himself in deep trouble, and tearing up the lives of others in the process.

Longarm listened to the exchange between Wes and the two citizens across the street from the saloon, then watched as Hardy descended the porch steps. He did not fail to notice as well the way Hardy was forced to favor his shoulder as he walked. The surprising thing to Longarm was that Wes was able to move as well as he did.

Wes was almost to the hotel when Longarm drew his .44 and stepped out of the livery doorway.

"All right, Hardy," he called softly. "Hold it right there."

Hardy spun. "That you, Longarm?"

"It's me, all right."

"You ain't got no call to draw down on me. That barkeep in there tried to ventilate me because I wanted another beer."

"And you're sure another jury trial would clear you."

"You're goddamn right I am."

Longarm walked out of the shadow of the livery stable and started across the street toward Wes, his Colt gleaming in the moonlight. "It ain't that poor son of a bitch you just shot down I'm bringing you in for, Wes. It's that raid on Hightower's place you just pulled off."

"Hell!" Wes exploded angrily. "That weren't me! That was the Calico Kid."

Still moving toward Wes, Longarm chuckled. "You were just out there at Hightower's, were you—watching the Calico Kid? Is that why you're so sure who it was?"

Cursing in sudden fury, Wes darted for the alley alongside the hotel, getting off a wild shot as he dove into the shadows. Longarm returned Hardy's fire, then raced after the fleeing man. The alley's darkness fell

122

over Longarm and he pulled up, uncertain. Then he heard Hardy's pounding feet and cut around the hotel corner after him.

Keeping to the shadows close behind the hotel, Longarm edged carefully along, his gun at the ready. Hardy's running footsteps had ceased, which meant that the big man was crouched somewhere, waiting. Longarm kept going cautiously, unhappy that he could have been this sloppy in his apprehension of Wes Hardy.

From her hotel window, Annie had watched Wes Hardy enter the saloon. As soon as he was inside, she hurried downstairs, took Prince from the livery, and tied him to a porch railing in the alley behind the general store next to the hotel, after which she returned to her room to wait for Hardy to leave the saloon. She was still waiting by the window when she heard the muffled report of two gunshots coming from inside the saloon.

Swiftly, her eyes still on the saloon entrance below her, she strapped on her Colt and clapped on her floppy-brimmed hat. She was dressed as usual in men's riding boots, Levi's, and a checked cotton shirt. A white silk bandanna was knotted at her throat.

Wes Hardy appeared on the saloon porch and began shouting across the street to a couple of men who had been drawn by the gunfire. Slowly, carefully lifting the window, she heard Wes tell the men they had better see to the burial of the barkeep, then watched as he started from the saloon, obviously heading for the hotel.

She was grimly pleased to see Wes approaching the hotel. Hurrying from her room, she moved swiftly and lightly down the stairs to the hotel's small lobby. The desk clerk was asleep in his chair. The gunfire in the saloon had obviously not been enough to rouse him.

Descending to the lobby, Annie darted past the desk and into a doorway behind it. Judging Wes to be close to the hotel by this time, she lifted her bandanna so that it covered her face, all except her eyes, then drew her Colt and pulled her hatbrim down a mite lower.

As soon as Wes stomped in to wake the desk clerk and demand a room, Annie planned to greet him with a .44-40 slug in the chest. It was about time the murdering bastard got what was coming to him.

She was beginning to fidget when she heard Longarm's quiet, commanding voice. Frowning, she strained to hear and, cursing to herself, heard the lawman telling Wes that he was taking him in. She left the doorway, moved swiftly to the hotel door, and pushed it open a crack—and was just in time to see Wes fling a shot at Longarm as he turned and bolted into the alley beside the hotel.

The clerk woke up. "Hey, there!" he cried. "What're you doin' there?"

Ignoring him, Annie bolted past the front desk and down the hallway. Pushing open the rear door leading from the hotel, she raced through the darkness, crossed over to the alley behind the general store, and untied the horse. Swingin up into the saddle, she cantered out of the alley to the next street parallel to Main Street, and headed back around toward the rear of the hotel.

Longarm thought he caught a movement just beyond the next outhouse. He held up and waited a moment, then moved cautiously on up the alley. A gun's flash and report exploded the darkness ahead of him. The slug slammed into the shingle inches from his forehead. Dropping to the ground and crabbing sideways toward the outhouse, Longarm snapped off two quick shots.

With the outhouse as a shield, he stood up and flattened himself against the small building, and peeked around its corner. He saw nothing. He moved around behind the outhouse, stepping cautiously in the darkness. In a moment he had circled the outhouse and found nothing. He peered about him in the darkness, then moved back into the alley and, crouching low, continued on down it.

From behind him he heard, "Stop right there, lawman. I got you covered good and proper."

Longarm spun. Wes was not lying. He had caught Longarm flat-footed.

"Drop the shootin' iron," Wes commanded.

Wes's voice, Longarm noted, was weak, very weak, which was not surprising, considering what the man had been through. That he was still this effective at this late an hour amazed Longarm.

"I am not going to drop it, Wes," Longarm said. "I'm going to swing it up and fire. We're close enough so it doesn't look like either of us is going to walk away from this one."

"That's crazy, Longarm."

"What choice do I have?"

"Now, listen. I can deal. I have the cards. You leave me be and I'll tell you who the Calico Kid really is."

"I'm listening."

"Is it a deal, damn you?"

"I don't make deals with killers."

"All right then, damn you!"

But before he could fire, the night exploded with the sudden thunder of a horse's hooves. Both men spun in time to see the Calico Kid thundering down the alley toward them. Before either one could bring up his gun, a rope snaked out, settling over Wes Hardy's shoulder.

With a vicious yank, the big redhead was stretched length-wise as the Calico Kid flashed past the transfixed Long-arm, dragging the screaming, struggling Hardy.

Longarm raced after them. At the end of the alley, the slim rider cut his mount sharply, heading back to Main Street with Wes Hardy—no longer struggling or crying out—bouncing along behind. Digging hard, Longarm darted from the alley and was just in time to see the Calico Kid galloping back down Main Street past the hotel, the limp body of Wes Hardy plowing up a dark plume of dust as it sped along behind. Abreast of the hotel, the Calico Kid turned in the saddle and, without slowing, fired twice into Wes's body. Then the Kid re-leased the rope and galloped on out of town.

Longarm raised his Colt to fire, then let it fall. Aboard that streaking bay, the Calico Kid had vanished into the night.

As Longarm holstered his .44, a crowd of scantily clad townsmen surged from the darkness toward the torn piece of flesh lying face down in the dust of Main Street.

Pushing through the crowd, Longarm knelt beside Wes Hardy. Rolling the man over, he saw at once that this time the big fellow was not going to get up again. Wes's face had been torn up fearfully. The rope had settled finally about his thick neck, and appeared to have stretched it considerably. Wes's right arm had been torn from his shoulder and was being held in place only by his deerskin jacket.

Incredibly, Wes's eyes opened. For a moment they gazed blankly up at the night sky. Then Wes turned his bloody head and focused his eyes on Longarm.

"All right, Wes," Longarm said softly. "You were going to tell me who the Calico Kid was."

"Yeah." The bleeding parody of a face twisted into what was meant to be a smile.

"Tell me, Wes."

"We got a deal?"

"Sure."

"In my pocket . . . calico bandanna . . . took it myself."

Longarm dug into the side pocket of Wes's deerskin jacket and removed the calico bandanna from it. An excited murmur passed through the crowd encircling them. Longarm heard the sudden hushed whispers. Wes Hardy was the Calico Kid!

"Wes, where'd you get this?" Longarm demanded.

Again came that terrible smile.

"Don't you know . . . ?"

"What the hell do you mean? Of course I don't."

By this time Wes's voice had become a sibilant rasp. Longarm had to lean close as Wes struggled to reply.

"She . . . was nice," Wes managed. "Enjoyed her, too."

Then he died. Longarm straightened, his senses reeling. He had no idea what in hell Wes had been trying to tell him.

At least he didn't think he did.

Chapter 9

Pushing her bay to its limits, Annie rode hard from Cottonwood, heading for her ranch. She planned to hole up for a while to pull her nerves together, then move out for one last foray.

This action had told her something about herself and her situation she could no longer ignore. There was no way she would ever be able to hide her identity from Longarm. So far he did not know that Carl Reese had been her father, or that it was Carl who had built and stocked this horse ranch for her. But once he found out who she was, it would be a simple matter for him to figure out the identity of the Calico Kid. From that point on, she could expect no mercy from him.

He was an upright man who lived by the book. He

would not want to bring her in, but he would have no other choice. Justice was the only code he lived by.

But not vigilante justice.

And what she had just learned about herself was equally important. Killing Wes Hardy back there had satisfied her enormously. If the Calico Kid disappeared now, Howard Murphy would escape the lash of her fury, and he was the one who had started this fateful roll of the dice in the first place. It was he who had paid Wes Hardy to gun down her father. Of all those who had died because of Carl Reese's death, the owner of the Lazy M was the one who most deserved to suffer a like fate. And yet he remained free, his enormous wealth and standing in the county a perfect shield behind which he might very well escape justice.

If Longarm attempted to bring the rancher in, he would be cut down. How could he possibly go against Murphy's gang of cutthroats? Longarm had escaped Murphy's clutches once, but he might not be so lucky again. Murphy would not leave the killing of Longarm to a couple of old sourdoughs this time.

Satisfied that she knew what she had to do, at peace with herself at last, Annie relaxed. She expected nothing beyond the death of Howard Murphy. With that accomplished, she would die content.

Holding Prince to a canter, she rode on through the night.

Longarm arrived back at the Hightower farm early the next afternoon. He was greeted at the door by Asa Fuller and John Hightower. The farmer limped a little, but outside of that he appeared fit enough.

"Light and set a spell," Hightower said.

Longarm dismounted. One of Hightower's urchins

grabbed the reins from him and led the black into what remained of the barn. To Longarm's surprise, the family seemed to have been able to salvage a considerable portion of it, though the roof was gone completely now and the odor of burnt hay hung like a pall over the place. One fortunate result, Longarm noted ironically, was that this did much to overwhelm the much less pleasant smell of the pigpen behind the house.

"What luck did you have, Longarm?" Asa asked.

As he walked into the cabin with them, Longarm described to Asa and Hightower the grim events of the previous night. When he had finished, he was sitting at the table, a cup of hot coffee in his hand, looking across at two very grim-faced men.

"So the Calico Kid got away, did he?" Asa said.

"The real Calico Kid, yes. The phony one—Wes Hardy—was taken care of with a certain brutal finality." Longarm frowned. "He tried to tell me who the Calico Kid was, but I couldn't make it out."

"Hell, he probably didn't know himself."

"That might be it, all right."

"So what now?" Asa asked.

By that time the blonde Hightower girl was standing beside Asa's chair, her hand on his shoulder. Behind Hightower stood his grim, placid wife. Longarm looked at them for a moment and shrugged.

"I don't have much choice," he told them. "I figure you two will be safe from the Calico Kid, if you stick together, that is. That leaves just Howard Murphy of the Lazy M for me to go after."

"Why are you going after him?" Hightower asked.

"He tried to kill me, and he was the one who paid Wes Hardy to kill Reese."

"So he was the one who started this whole business."

"I guess that's the truth of it."

"I'm going with you," said Asa.

"Reckon I'll be goin' along, too," said Hightower.

"Now, listen here. You two don't need to do anything of the kind."

"Hell, we know that," said Asa.

"Fill your belly first," said Hightower. "Then we'll move out." He smiled wolfishly. "I always hated that high-steppin' son of a bitch. Every time I borrowed one of his cows, his riders would come down on me real hard. As if he was gonna miss some mangy cow he'd already rustled from some other poor devil."

This was the longest speech Longarm had ever heard from Hightower. It was a measure, therefore, of his resentment of Howard Murphy and his determination to join forces with Longarm. With a shrug, Longarm accepted and leaned back, perfectly willing for Mrs. Hightower to fill his belly.

Joanna Rawlings gazed at herself in the mirror. If she could do something about her gray hair, she would be completely satisfied. Having just returned from a shopping trip to Denver, she was trying on one of the dresses she had purchased. It was a spring green with lace at the throat and the elbows. It was cut nicely, hugging her bosom and hips, then flaring gracefully to her ankles. The latest style, the saleslady had assured her.

She spun quickly in front of the mirror and uttered a deep, contented sigh. Yes, Howard Murphy was a considerably better match for her than Bill had ever been. Or that animal Wes Hardy.

Still, even now, recalling the awesome appetite of that brute set her to tingling all over. For a while she had allowed herself to drink deep from Hardy's wild, satanic brew. The pain and even the baseness of it had carried her to heights she had never expected to climb, astonishing and exhilarating her, allowing her to shed finally, like dead skin, the irksome restraints bred into her by a grim, passionless upbringing. For that she would always be grateful to Wes Hardy. At least he knew what a woman was for—if the woman had the courage to admit it to herself.

She shuddered deliciously, then caught herself. She must put Hardy out of her thoughts and be content with this one. Howard was strong enough, and his appetite almost as powerful as Hardy's, and he fed and clothed her better than any man she had ever known before. If he treated her somewhat coldly—as if she were something he had bought and paid for at a cattle auction— she would simply have to accept this as the price she must pay for his occasional indulgences, such as this recent trip to Denver.

She stepped out of the green dress and hurried over to the bed for the red gown with the black lace trim, the one with the low-cut bodice that Howard had insisted she buy. The door opened and Howard entered. He chuckled when he saw her in just her corset and chemise.

"Just in time, am I?"

She turned boldly to him, not attempting any false modesty by holding the green dress up in front of her. "In time for what?" she asked calmly, her eyes glowing with a sudden fire.

"You know damn well what I mean," he said, smiling. "Take off that armor, woman. It's time for you to thank me for all these goodies."

"Of course," she said.

Her fingers trembled slightly as she began unfastening the hooks and eyes that bound her.

* * *

The three riders topped the ridge and gazed down at
Snake Draw. The stream bed that wound through it was
not yet completely dry, but the cottonwoods that shaded
it looked as tired and as thirsty as they felt.

Longarm glanced at his two deputies. "I'll camp down
there tonight and stay until Murphy's men discover me.
Each of you find a spot on this ridge. Make sure you've
got a good enough view of the campfire I'll keep going.
But remember, when night comes, that won't be me you
see curled up alongside it."

"How about us filling our canteens?" Asa asked, his
pale face appearing even more gaunt than when he had
started out three days earlier.

"Mine, too," said John Hightower.

"Take all you want. It's free, even if it is on Lazy M
land. But get yourself hidden as soon as you can. We
don't know when one of Murphy's riders will discover
my camp. We might already have been spotted."

Asa stood up in his saddle, the good leather of it
creaking. His cold eyes turned to slits as he scanned the
horizon in all directions. "I don't think so," he said. "Not
a speck of dust was raised this day, and I would have
seen any riders who got close enough to see us. Murphy's
riders are staying well out of this heat, I'm thinking."

Longarm nodded. That was what he had figured, too.
"Let's get on down there." he said, angling his chestnut
down the steep slope that led into the draw. "Those trees
and that water look real inviting."

It was later that same day when Jeeter saw the thin tracery
of smoke coming from the direction of Snake Draw. He
had been ordered to round up any strays he could find

and drive them over to the north flat, where there was still good water.

By this time, he had gathered about ten head and was hazing them toward the north flat. His first thought when he caught sight of the smoke was to ride back to the main house and alert Gil. The foreman could then check with the old man to see what they should do. They had standing orders to keep track of anyone found on Lazy M land. But if he left this gather to return to the main house, these ten head would scatter once again, and he didn't relish doing this job all over again tomorrow.

He decided he would drive his bunch over to the draw and investigate himself. There should be enough water left in the draw for the beef, so he would be killing two birds with one stone. He would probably find some sodbusters on their way through to the mountains using the draw for an overnight campsite. Jeeter would take real pleasure sending them on their way a little sooner than they had planned.

It was considerably later than Jeeter had anticipated when he finally approached the ridge overlooking Snake Draw. He never could get used to how deceptively close truly distant landmarks appeared in this high country. He took out his canteen and drank deep, the cattle crowding ahead of him over the ridge, stumbling and brawling their way down into the draw. They had smelled the water long before he had.

Topping the ridge, he pulled up, screwed the cap back onto his canteen, and peered down into the draw, searching for any sign of a camp. He found it at once, on the far side of the stream under a particularly big cottonwood. A lone cowpoke was standing up beside the tree, shading his eyes as he peered up the steep slope at the cattle spilling down toward him.

Hell, just a lone cowboy lost on Murphy's land, Jeeter realized. It wouldn't take much to set fire to his britches. Smiling meanly, he put away his canteen, snatched up his reins, and started down the slope after the cattle.

Longarm stood his ground as the Lazy M rider angled his horse down the slope. Not until the rider had reached the rocky stream bed did he move back into the cotton-woods. The rider splashed across the narrow rivulet that still flowed through the draw, scattering his gather ahead of him. Gaining the near bank, the rider pulled up, chucked his hat back off his head, and grinned.

Peering at him through the trees, Longarm waited, his sixgun out.

"All right, mister!" the puncher called. "Come out of there! You're on Lazy M land! That's trespassin'!"

"Come and get me!" Longarm called, disguising his voice slightly.

"Dammit! I'll come in there and get you and I'll whup your britches, too. I told you! You're on Lazy M land!"

"I don't care if it's God Almighty's land!" Longarm called back. "I'm camping here as long as I want. And just maybe I might file a homestead claim while I'm at it!"

"You'll what?" the puncher exploded, his face turning purple at the suggestion.

"You heard me!" Longarm retorted. "Now get them cows out of here—and you, too!"

With an oath, the puncher pulled his hat down, drew his iron, and charged the cottonwoods where Longarm was crouching. Aiming carefully at the foolish rider, he fired. His aim was excellent. The puncher's hat went flying back off his head. Only its chin strap kept it from spinning to the ground. Another shot whispered close over the puncher's head. The puncher obviously heard it, judging from the way he ducked frantically down and reined in his horse.

"Hey now!" the rider cried. "We can talk this over!"

"We've done talking, cowpoke! You and your cows get out of here!"

"Damn it!" the puncher responded in a perfect fury. "These ain't cows, these are beef cattle. They belong to the Lazy M!"

This time, instead of responding verbally, Longarm aimed carefully and sent up a small geyser of mud and gravel just in front of the puncher's mount. As the round ricochetted past the horse's forelegs, the animal reared, its big eyes rolling in its head. The puncher had all he could do to keep from being thrown.

"Get out of here while you still can!" Longarm called to him through the trees. "And thanks for all this beef. I'll just help myself."

The puncher wheeled his mount and charged back up the slope. He did not spare his horse and twice the animal went down. Rowelling his horse with a zeal born of terror and fury, the puncher continued on over the ridge and disappeared from sight.

Stepping out from the cottonwoods, Longarm grinned coldly, glanced with some appreciation down at his .44, then holstered it. Asa and Hightower materialized beside him.

Holstering his two gleaming revolvers, Asa looked admiringly at the lawman. "That was a real fine exhibition, Longarm. It's been a long time since I've seen that kind of shooting."

"Just so long as he brings a crowd."

"Oh, hell," laughed Asa. "He should do that, all right. You agree, John?"

"Yup," said Hightower, hefting his Hawken.

It was night when Jeeter rode, flat out, into the Lazy M compound. He threw himself from his horse while it was still moving, paying no attention at all to its foam-flecked flanks. He had almost caused the mount to founder, and that was not a good practice on this ranch. But all he could think of was getting back to that draw with the boys to eat that squatter alive.

"Gil! Red! Lance!" he called, running toward the bunkhouse.

At once the bunkhouse door was flung open, spilling yellow lantern light onto the hard-packed ground. Gil Dugan strode out, the rest of the crew crowding after him.

"What in hell is it?" Gil demanded, pulling up in front of Jeeter. "You gone loco or something?"

Jeeter shook his head emphatically. "It ain't me's gone loco. We got ourselves a squatter in Snake Draw. He's plumb crazy. He fired at me a dozen times and drove me off. Said he was going to claim a quarter section near the stream and help himself to our beef."

"Hell!" exploded the foreman. "You makin' this up?"

"Now why in hell would I do that, Gil?" Jeeter asked in a fever of frustration. He whipped off his hat and thrust it at Gil. "Look at that hole in the rim!"

Gil saw the hole, then passed the hat to the men crowding close around them. "Okay. It's a fresh bullet hole. You say this squatter took a shot at you?"

"Hell, it wasn't just *one* shot!"

"That's right. You said he fired at you a dozen times. He sure as hell must have been a lousy shot if he missed you after all that."

"Well, now, thunderation and hellfire, Gil! I didn't

138

just sit my horse and let that son of a bitch fire at me. I fired back, kept moving in, trying to get a bead on him. But he kept himself hid in the cottonwoods, as slick as a phantom."

Gil reached out and lifted Jeeter's iron from its holster. He placed his hand around the barrel, and grinned at Jeeter. Then he inspected the fully loaded cylinders, after which he glanced at Jeeter's full cartridge belt.

He chuckled. "You say you exchanged shots with this feller?"

"Dammit, Gil," Jeeter said, snatching back his weapon. "You goin' to believe what I told you or not? We got a squatter in Snake Draw and he's fired on a Lazy M rider. And he's stealin' our cattle!"

"I guess I believe you," said Gil, serious now. "Ain't nothing else I know of could make you this agitated— or make you punish a horse that bad," he added, glancing past Jeeter at the drooping animal, which had stumbled to a halt in the middle of the compound.

A shout came from above. They looked up and saw Murphy, dressed in a ruby-colored bathrobe, standing on the balcony and resting his hands on the railing as he glared down at them. "What in hell's this ruckus all about?" he demanded.

They saw the figure of his new woman approaching him from behind. She was wearing a filmy white nightgown and it was plain to each man staring up at them what sweet activity Jeeter's sudden, raucous alarm had interrupted.

"We got a squatter!" Gil cried. "He's camping in Snake Draw. Jeeter say's he's eatin' our beef."

"And he fired on me!" Jeeter cried.

"He's defying the Lazy M, looks like," Gil said.

"One man?" Murphy asked. "He must be crazy."

"What do you want us to do?" Gil asked.

"Hell, you know better than to ask me that! Ride out there and string the son of a bitch up! And do it now!"

His arm about Joanna's waist, Murphy swung around and disappeared back through the French doors leading to the master bedroom. Every man on the ground watching them felt a sick envy gnawing at his vitals.

Looking away, Gil took a deep breath. He had been ready to turn in, but he preferred riding at night to riding during the day, at least in this kind of weather. He peered around him at the circle of faces.

"Lance, Slim, Mel, Red, Jeeter—you'll be riding back to Snake Draw with me. Tompkins, you stay behind with Jake, Pete, and Nate to keep an eye on things. You'll be in charge." He grinned suddenly. "See that you don't disturb the old man."

Tompkins nodded solemnly. He always got left behind. He wasn't too old to ride, he only looked that way.

"All right, boys," Gil said, "saddle up. We got a long ride ahead of us—and a damned squatter to punish when we get there."

It was close to midnight when Longarm heard the first faint thunder of many hooves. Asa and Hightower heard it at about the same time. The three of them were on the ridge overlooking the draw, where they had been waiting since the puncher hightailed it out of the draw.

"I'll get down there," Longarm said, "and pile some more wood on the fire. You fellers know what to do."

"Yup," said Hightower.

"Sounds like a small army," remarked Asa grimly, as he lifted both his revolvers from their holsters and checked their load.

"That's what we're hoping for, at least," agreed Longarm. "This ought to be a perfect way to test that axiom that surprise in battle is worth an extra division."

"Hell," said Asa, "I never heard that one."

"Neither did I," admitted Longarm with a grim. "But it sure has a nice ring to it."

"You goin' to build up that fire?" Hightower asked, standing up to peer in the direction from which the sound was coming.

The muffled thunder of pounding hooves was no longer so muffled as it had been. As Longarm scanned the dark horizon he thought he glimpsed a dim, moving shape— a crowd of horsemen, perhaps.

Without another word, Longarm angled his long form down the slope, pushing past the Lazy M cattle when he reached the gully floor. The campfire was glowing brightly, and after a few judicious pokes with a branch, Longarm got the flames to dancing again. He fed the flames with bone-dry firewood and the fire was soon crackling merrily.

After piling still more wood on the fire, he turned his attention to the dummy he had placed close by the campfire. He had constructed it of boulders, his saddle, and a bedroll, with his hat completing the deception. Now, in the campfire's shifting light, Longarm himself found it difficult to believe that it was not himself he saw curled up by the fire, asleep.

He moved into the rocks above the campfire and waited.

"There!" Jeeter said, pointing down at the campfire, winking like Satan's eye in the gully below them. The rocks and trees surrounding the fire, including the bulky shapes of the Lazy M's cattle, trembled in the dancing flames.

Pulling up beside Jeeter, Gil Dugan stared down at the campfire and at the figure sleeping beside it. "He's a brazen bastard, ain't he," the foreman muttered. "He ain't makin' no effort to stay hid."

"He's a bloody wild man, the kind that feeds on trouble, I'm thinking," said Slim Wiley, coming to a halt on the other side of the foreman. "I know the type. Likes to chew nails before breakfast, just to keep his hand in."

"We'll show 'im," said Red, grinning. He had his knife out and was sharpening its gleaming blade on his thigh. The sound of the blade snicking across his Levi's came clearly to each of them as they peered down at the campfire.

"What're we waiting for?" complained Jeeter. "Let's go get the son of a bitch."

Gil took a deep breath and continued to peer down at the campfire's dancing flames. Then he studied the cottonwoods and the rocks surrounding it. An uncertain, troubled wariness fell over him.

"I don't like it," he said. "It's too pat. You say he ran you off, Jeeter? Fired at you?"

"You doubtin' my word?"

"Sure I am, for Christ's sake. Where the hell do you think I'd be now if I believed every story you saddle tramps told me? What's bothering me is this: if that squatter down there ran you off, why isn't he on guard? How come he's all curled up nice and cozy in front of his campfire, suspecting nothing? I tell you, I don't like it."

"Shit, Gil," said Slim, "that ain't hard to understand. Like I said, this fellow is so damn sure of himself, he don't think he needs to take precautions. He's like Wes Hardy. Hell, you ever hear that joke—where's a two-ton grizzly sleep?"

"Anywhere he likes," acknowledged Gil, still staring gloomily down into the draw.

"Let's go," urged Jeeter.

"If you're so anxious," said Gil, "you lead the way."

"All right, dammit. I will!"

Exhibiting a bravado he did not feel, Jeeter clapped spurs to his horse and plunged on down the slope, the rest following in single file. Gil would have preferred that they spread out and come at the squatter from all sides, but he found it difficult to get himself too worked up over a single squatter so dumb that he had curled himself up alongside his blazing campfire on Lazy M land.

The suddenly skittish cattle on the floor of the draw gave Jeeter some difficulty as he threaded his way through them. It was as black as the inside of a whore's heart below the ridge, with only the flickering light from the campfire to show him the way. Heading toward it now, sixgun drawn and ready, he kept his eye on the sleeping figure. He had decided he would not fire on the son of a bitch while he was still sleeping.

But as soon as the bastard sat up and went for his iron, Jeeter was going to fill his carcass with lead.

Jeeter reached the wash. His mount's shoes clicked loudly on the stones that filled it. Jeeter tensed, waiting for the sleeper to leap up. Behind him, one of the horses shook its head and blew. Unaccountably, the sleeping figure remained as still as a statue. Closer and still closer Jeeter rode, his heart thudding in his throat.

The flames leaped momentarily higher. In that instant, Jeeter thought he caught a flash of movement from the squatter, and with it the gleam of a sixgun. Without waiting a second longer, Jeeter flung up his sixgun and began firing. As if on command, the others fanned out and began firing at the sleeping figure as well. But the only response they got was the whine of their bullets as they ricocheted off the sleeper's form.

"Oh, shit!" Jeeter cried to the others as the dummy's hat went flying. "It's a trap!"

Gil cried, "Let's get the hell out of here!"

But it was too late. From the rocks above them, a shot exploded. Jeeter felt a slug tear into his arm. Crying out in pain and terror, he flung himself off his horse. Then from the slope behind them came more fire. Mel cried out and slid from his horse. Gil, wheeling his animal, tried to bull his way back through the milling cattle, but a shot from the cottonwoods caught him in the side, knocking him from his mount.

Red saw at once that they were fighting more than one man and realized that Jeeter had led them into a trap. He dove from his horse, kept low, and began scrambling for cover in the rocks. His knife was out and his eyes were searching for gun flashes. He caught one high in the rocks off to his left and veered for it. He would get one of them anyway, he told himself.

Behind Red, Lance cried out, "Stop firing! I'm done for! Stop firing!"

Lance's call was swiftly echoed by Jeeter and the others. Even Gil Dugan cried out. Muttering furiously to himself at this weakness, Red slipped higher into the rocks. Just above him now, he could make out a dim figure, a sixgun gleaming in his hand.

In answer to the men's cries, the firing from the cottonwoods and the rocks ceased. All Red could hear now was the faint bawling of the cattle and the moans of the wounded men. Skirting widely about the figure on the slope, he came out above him and crept closer.

Longarm stood up and shouted down to the Lazy M

riders, "Get over to the fire so we can see you. Then toss your weapons up here into the rocks."

With sullen curses, the men began complying. Some were forced to crawl, while others were able to limp closer to the fire unaided. One man, a tall, slim fellow who had obviously escaped injury, helped some of his severely wounded companions to make it into the ring of light created by the campfire. Longarm counted five men, and was immediately on the alert. He had seen six Lazy M riders plunging down that slope toward the campfire.

It was Howard Murphy Longarm wanted, and the possibility that his ruse had not succeeded in drawing the Lazy M owner out to this draw dismayed him. But there was still the chance that the missing sixth rider might be Murphy.

Longarm stood up. "Asa!" he called. "Hightower! Keep an eye out. There's only five riders down there, and there should be six. One of them is missing. It might be Murphy!"

"Get down, then!" shouted Asa from the slope to Longarm's left.

What sounded like the rowel of a spur struck a rock just behind him. In that instant Longarm realized how dangerous it was to take anything for granted. He spun. A hulking figure loomed over him, a knife gleaming in his upraised hand. Twisting swiftly away to one side, Longarm felt himself falling. But even as he did, he was bringing up his double-action .44, pumping round after round into the figure above him.

His back slammed into the ground, and he went tumbling ass over teakettle down the steep slope. Sore and considerably bruised, he scrambled to his feet at the bottom of the slope, stepping aside in time to miss the tumbling form of the man he had just ventilated. Coming to rest a few feet beyond Longarm, the big fellow lay heavily on the rocks.

As Longarm bent over the silent hulk, Hightower and Asa broke across the draw toward him. Longarm turned the man over. In the flickering light from the campfire, he saw a burly smashed face topped with red hair. He did not recognize him and, with a bitter curse, he stood up to face Asa and Hightower as they pulled to a halt before him.

"Dammit! He's not Murphy!"

"Then he must still be back at his ranch," said Asa.

Longarm looked back down at the dead man. He had sure as hell guessed wrong. He had not thought that anything could have kept the owner of the Lazy M from dealing personally with a squatter on his land. He had fully expected to see Murphy himself leading his riders.

"What now?" asked Asa.

"We'll have to go after him."

Hightower said nothing. He just shifted the rifle in his arms and sent a long shaft of tobacco juice to the ground.

Chapter 10

Annie Reese pulled up in some astonishment. Expecting the Lazy M compound to be swarming with Murphy's hands, she had dismounted on the far side of a ridge overlooking the ranch and had waited until nightfall, counting on the cover of darkness to enable her to enter the big house.

Now—almost on cue, it seemed—most of Murphy's riders were galloping out of the compound, a dark cloud of horsemen riding as if the devil himself were lashing at their flanks. Where they could be going in such an all-fired hurry at this hour scarcely interested Annie. It was enough for her that the way was now clear.

Mounting quickly, she rode across the prairie toward the dark huddle of buildings. She was no longer the Calico Kid. This time there would be no calico bandanna, no swift bay. She was going to enter the ranch as Annie

147

Reese, Carl Reese's daughter, come to see the great Howard Murphy, rich cattleman and empire builder. He had never met her, and she was not sure her father had ever let on to the owner of the Lazy M—as he evidently had to Wes Hardy—that he had a daughter. But that did not matter. Murphy would know soon enough.

She took her bay through the gates at a walk. Once into the compound, the only lights she saw were coming from the bunkhouse. Dismounting, she looked carefully about her. The unexpected absence of most of Murphy's riders had radically altered the odds. She saw possibilities now that had not occurred to her earlier.

Leading her horse around behind the bunkhouse, she tied it up securely to a porch railing. She glanced into one of the bunkhouse windows and saw only four men, all of them rather old, none of them very threatening in appearance. The oldest was a bent stick of a man; another appeared to be nursing a broken wrist. It was clear that the best of Murphy's riders had just galloped out through the gate.

She left the window and knocked on the bunkhouse door.

Slow steps approached it from the other side. She took out her Colt and waited patiently. The door was pulled open. It was the oldest puncher. When he saw the Colt in her hand, he tried to pull back in a hurry. He only succeeded in giving his head a nasty crack as he struck the doorjamb.

"Now, what in tarnation—" the old puncher cried, his wide, startled eyes fixed on the Colt's muzzle.

Shoving the Colt into his gut, Annie pushed him ahead of her back into the bunkhouse. When the other three saw what was happening, they jumped up, their eyes as wide as saucers.

"Say, lookee here," said one of them, starting toward her. He was the youngest of the oldtimers, a skinny fellow with thinning gray hair and milky blue eyes. "You better put that shootin' iron down, ma'am!"

Moving swiftly away from the old puncher, Annie cocked the Colt and pointed it at the one coming toward her. Her voice cold, she told him, "I want you to tie your friends up. And do a good job of it. I'll crack your skull with the barrel of this Colt if you don't."

"Aw, hell, ma'am," he protested. "You wouldn't do a thing like that."

He reached out his bony hand to take the weapon from her. The other two started for her, as well.

With an unhappy shrug, Annie stepped back to the old puncher and brought the barrel of her sixgun down on his head. The oldtimer crumpled to the floor with a sigh like that of a horse being relieved of a heavy saddle.

"Does that convince you?" she asked, covering the rest of them.

The skinny one swallowed and backed up hastily. "There's some rawhide on the wall there," he told her. "I'll get it."

"Do that."

The other two sat with sullen docility as the skinny fellow, under Annie's watchful eye, trussed them up securely. She allowed the fellow with the broken wrist to keep his wrist free, but saw to it that his arm was bound tightly behind him.

"Now it's your turn," Annie said to the skinny one when he had finished trussing up his companions.

The man nodded unhappily.

"Turn around."

"Please, ma'am..."

"Turn around, goddammit!"

He turned.

Stepping swiftly forward, she brought the barrel of her Colt down on the crown of his head. He slumped crookedly to the floor. As soon as he was still, she trussed him and the first one she had knocked out as securely as she could. Then, stuffing their mouths with pillowcases, she hurried from the bunkhouse.

She looked around for something to jam up against the bunkhouse door and came upon a rotting fence post lying on the ground. Dragging it over to the bunkhouse, she propped it securely against the door and took a quick look around to make sure she had not been spotted. The compound was deserted. Not a figure moved in the darkness. The only sound came from the restless stamping of the horses in the barn and the distant call of nighthawks.

Her gaze came to rest on the magnificent house that dominated the compound, its whitewashed walls shimmering in the moonlight. At that moment she realized that what she wanted almost as much as Murphy's death was to see to it that the last thing the cattleman glimpsed before he died was the complete destruction of his world.

She ran lightly across the yard to the barn and released into the rear corral the horses and other livestock stabled there. Then she opened the corrals and drove the horses out into the fields. Shaking their heads and arching their necks in pleasure, the horses pranced out into the night, the few calves and mules following after them. She emptied the other two barns as well, then reached down a lantern from a hook, lit it, and broke it against the wall. In seconds the flames had leapt into the haymow. Darting into the adjoining barns, she set them afire as well, then raced back across the compound.

Letting herself into the big house through the kitchen,

she picked up a lamp, lit it, then used it to find the front staircase. She mounted the stairs softly, her Colt in one hand, the lamp in the other. When she reached the second floor, she paused, uncertain as to which door led to the master bedroom.

She waited a moment, then fired a shot into the air. As plaster sifted down from the ceiling, a glow from a lamp shone under a door halfway down the hall. She headed for it, but before she reached the door, Howard Murphy flung it open.

"What the hell—" he cried when he saw Annie. "Was that you fired that shot?"

"It was," said Annie, waggling her revolver at the man. "Get back into that room. I have something to show you."

"Now, hold it right there, ma'am! And stop waggling that cannon at me! It might go off."

She aimed swiftly and fired, splintering the floor at his feet. He danced frantically back, his eyes suddenly wide with terror.

"I told you," she repeated, "get back in that room. I have something to show you."

This time Murphy obeyed. Annie followed him in. The lamp Murphy had lit was sitting on a nightstand beside his bed. Sitting up in the bed, naked from the waist up, was Joanna Rawlings. She was as surprised and startled as Murphy, but all she revealed was a sullen fury at this unwelcome intrusion.

Annie placed the lamp she was carrying down beside her on top of a chest of drawers. "Turn around," she told Murphy, "and step out onto that balcony of yours."

"Now, listen here!" the rancher demanded. "This is my home! You can't come in here like this!"

Annie sent two bullets through one of the French

doors, bringing down the drawn curtains and shattering the windowpanes. The glow from the burning barns came through the shattered doors, transforming the bedroom into a garish, flickering hell.

"My God!" Murphy gasped, spinning to look out. "The barns are going up!"

Joanna snatched up a gown, threw back her covers, and hurried to his side. One glance and she turned on Annie. "You did this!"

"Yes!"

Murphy spun to face her. "Why?" he demanded. "Who are you?"

"Carl Reese's daughter."

Murphy groaned.

"Now go on out there onto that fancy balcony of yours," Annie told him. "I want you to watch those barns go up first."

"You're not serious!"

"Were you serious when you paid Wes Hardy to kill my father?"

"Did he tell you that? My God, woman! You can't believe that murderer! Wes killed Carl on his own. I had nothing to do with it!"

"I don't believe you."

"It's true!"

"Wes Hardy was the murderer? You are convinced of that, are you?"

"Of course! There was never any doubt about that."

"And you were on the jury that tried Wes?"

"Yes, I was."

She smiled coldly. "And so you voted to acquit him."

Murphy's face broke. It was clear to him then that there was no way he could reach Annie. He was a dead man.

"Go on now," Annie told him. "Step out there and watch those barns burn."

"I'd rather not."

Annie fired carefully at Murphy, catching him in his left elbow. The bullet's impact spun him to the floor. He sat there, clutching his arm, staring up at Annie in disbelief.

"You heard me," Annie told him, calmly reloading her Colt. "Go on out onto that balcony."

"Please—" Murphy cried, his voice breaking. "There must be some way we can work this..."

Annie's next shot caught him in the foot, spinning him violently about on the floor, causing him to sprawl face down in a widening pool of his own blood.

"All right, then," Annie said. "Stay where you are."

She picked up the lamp she had set down and flung it at the wall over the bed. It shattered, and with a sudden *whomp* sent tongues of fire up the wall and down across the bedspread.

Shrieking, Joanna rushed at Annie. Not wanting to hurt her, Annie tried to fend her off. But before she was aware of what was happening, Annie felt something sharp and paralyzing slipping deep into her chest under her right breast. For a moment she had difficulty catching her breath. Flinging Joanna from her, she looked down.

What she saw was the pearl button of one of Joanna's hatpins protruding from her cotton shirt. She yanked the bloodstained hatpin out and flung it across the room.

"I ought to kill you!" Annie told Joanna, finding it suddenly difficult to speak and breathe easily. "Go on, now. Get out of here while you still can."

The flames were lapping across the ceiling and one entire wall was enveloped in flames. Joanna cowered back. "But... what about Howard?"

"He's staying right here. Now get out!"

The searing heat made further argument impossible. Covering her gray hair with both hands, Joanna ducked low and fled from the room. Annie looked back at Murphy. The man was groaning softly as he writhed on the floor.

Hurrying over to him, she grabbed one of his arms, kicked open the shattered French door, and dragged him out onto the balcony. The towering sheets of flame billowing up from the burning barns had turned night into day. Smaller outbuildings were catching fire as well, some from the burning embers that landed on their roofs, others bursting into fire simply from the intense heat. Only the bunkhouse appeared safe from the conflagration.

Annie began to cough. Reaching up to her mouth, she felt a small trickle of blood coming from one corner.

Murphy groaned. He wasn't dead. Not yet. Behind them, the room was a seething cauldron of flames. Shielding her face from the searing heat, she aimed carefully so as not to kill him outright, and squeezed off a shot, catching him in the small of the back. He cried out when the round entered his spine, then flopped over, cowering up at her in horror.

"You'll burn, Murphy!" she told him. "This is your hellfire!"

"Damn you!" he cried hoarsely. "Damn you to hell!"

She smiled grimly down at the dying man. "Maybe we'll meet there," she told him, "and finish this."

Holstering her gun, she climbed over the balcony railing, hung by her hands for a moment, then dropped to the ground. She lit lightly and should have had no trouble regaining her feet, but dizziness momentarily hampered her. Shaking it off, she hurried around behind the bunkhouse to her horse and mounted up.

Without a single glance back at the inferno piling into the heavens behind her, she rode out through the blazing compound and headed for her ranch in the hills.

The glow from the burning ranch lit the southern sky. It was Asa who saw it first. He called Longarm and Hightower up onto the ridge and pointed it out to them.

"What do you make of that?"

"Fire," said Hightower.

"I know that, dammit! But is that a prairie fire, or buildings?"

"It's staying in one place," said Longarm. "Like a big bonfire. I'd say it was buildings. A ranch maybe."

"Hell, ain't the Lazy M in that direction?"

"It is."

"Maybe we better hurry, then."

"Perhaps," said Longarm, "it doesn't matter any more if we do or not."

"Now, what in blazes do you mean by that?"

"I'm not sure I know myself. All right. Those men down there are as comfortable as we can make them. Let's get this over with."

Mounting up, the three men galloped toward the glowing horizon.

It was a few moments past the first light of day when Longarm and the others rode into the Lazy M compound.

The fires had subsided considerably, and by this time, Longarm and the others were fully aware that they no longer had anything to fear from Howard Murphy or his men. They pulled up in the middle of the compound and, with some surprise, watched Joanna Rawlings hurry across the compound toward them. Four old lazy M hands were close behind her. They appeared totally exhausted. One of them had a filthy bandage wound around his head; another was resting a broken wrist inside his shirt front. It was obvious that all of them had waged a battle that had thoroughly demoralized them. Losing battles usually did.

Dismounting, Longarm touched the brim of his hat to Joanna. She was wearing only a long nightgown. It was torn at the hem and there were dark smudges across the front of it. Her gray hair was wild, her eyes even wilder as she pulled up before Longarm.

"You're Marshal Long!" she cried.

"Yes, ma'am," he said. "I've come for Howard Murphy."

"This way," she said, turning swiftly. "We tried to save him before the flames reached him, but..." With an unhappy shake of her head, she said no more.

She led them toward the blackened shell of what had once been one of the largest, most impressive houses in the country. Asa and Hightower kept behind Longarm, the sad contingent of elderly Lazy M riders following at a discreet distance.

Under a cottonwood behind the house, Howard Murphy had been propped up beside a rain barrel. From his waist up, he had been wrapped in bandages, and one leg and one arm were also bandaged. What portions of his anatomy were not swathed in bandages were a mass of torn, blackened strips, but Longarm could not tell if these strips were burnt clothing or peeling skin.

It was not yet fully light, and in the shadow of the tree, Longarm had difficulty making out Murphy's face. It was still as flushed and as ruddy as Longarm remembered it, but his gray hair was no longer visible. Frowning suddenly, Longarm held up and looked closer. To his horror, he saw that Murphy's eyes and nose were gone completely. Longarm felt his stomach flip. He turned quickly away, then braced himself and forced himself to look back at the raw piece of beefsteak that had once been a man's face.

"Who's that?" Murphy asked. "Who's there? That you, Joanna?"

She hurried to his side. "Yes," she told him. "It's me. The deputy marshal is here."

"Marshal!" the man cried, looking blindly about him, his voice rising to no more than a hoarse whisper. "Marshal! You must go after her. You must find her. She did this."

Asa and Hightower keeping pace with him, Longarm moved still closer to the ravaged cattleman.

"She?" he asked in some bafflement. "Who do you mean?"

"That girl! Carl Reese's daughter!"

Longarm found it difficult to follow the man. "You mean...a woman did *this?*"

"Yes, damn your eyes! A woman! Came clear out of hell to do this to me!"

He began to cough weakly. Everyone waited. It was like watching a very unpleasant animal perform a nasty function. But no one turned his head away. The fascination was too great. Gradually, the man's coughing subsided.

"Marshal!" he called, his voice little more than a whisper now. "Come closer."

Longarm knelt beside the man and found himself looking into two holes that had once, he remembered, held two very sharp, alert brown eyes. "I'm right here," he told Murphy.

"She deliberately sent a bullet through my spine,"

Murphy told Longarm. "That's why I can't get up. But I escaped her hellfire. I dragged myself through it!" What remained of his face grimaced in sudden pain. He turned blindly toward Joanna. "It's getting worse," he rasped. "Water, please!"

Joanna nodded to one of the hands. He hurried over to the rain barrel and, as Longarm moved quickly back out of the way, began ladling great, splashing gobs of water down over Murphy's skull. Longarm almost thought he could see steam rising from the cattleman's head and shoulders.

Longarm glanced down then to look more closely at the man's bare arm and leg and thigh. The black, scorched strips he had noticed were not burnt clothing—they were what remained of Murphy's skin. Beneath the strips, visible through layers of soot and ash, gleamed the lobster red of muscle and sinew.

Howard Murphy was a dead man. The real horror was that he had lasted this long. It would be a kindness if someone would give him a gun.

Joanna got to her feet also and came over to Longarm.

"He hasn't long," he said to her softly, taking her gently by the arm and leading her away from the tree.

"I know."

"You married him?"

"In Denver two days ago. We were on our honeymoon."

"Tell me about this girl."

"She told him she was Carl Reese's daughter."

"I did not know Reese had a daughter."

"Neither did Howard."

"Can you describe her to me?"

"Small, slender, long blonde hair. Boyish, I'd say. I . . . tried to hurt her, but it was no use."

"Did you see her ride off?"

"Yes."

"Which direction did she take?"

"West, toward the mountains."

"I should tell you this: I rode in here just now to arrest Howard Murphy for jury tampering and for hiring Wes Hardy to murder Carl Reese—and for trying to have me murdered, as well. Most of my witnesses are dead now, but I fully expected trouble from Murphy anyway, and was looking forward to giving it back to him in spades. Do you get my meaning?"

She looked at him coldly. "Yes. You intended to kill him."

"I was hoping for such an opportunity, yes. Now there's another matter. The dead body of one Lazy M rider and five others, four of them wounded, are in Snake Draw. We bound them securely to keep them there while we rode over here. If you are now the owner of the Lazy M, I suggest you see to them. You will need their help to rebuild the Lazy M."

"I'll send Tompkins," she said, her eyes suddenly growing alert.

Perhaps, Longarm surmised, Joanna had not realized until that moment what she would inherit with her new husband's death. The land and the cattle still remained. She could build anew, and this time her own way.

"Joanna!" one of the hands cried, hurrying toward her. "You better come now!"

Watching her hurry to her dying husband's side, Longarm remained where he was. He had seen enough this day to last a lifetime. Asa and Hightower joined him. Both of the men looked as bad as Longarm felt.

"Let's ride," Longarm said. "Our business is finished here."

They galloped out of the fire-ravaged compound, past sad little fires still winking in the corners of ruined structures, away from the stench of burned things that clung to them now like a curse.

But, the smell of death followed Longarm. For, as he recalled Howard Murphy's ravaged face, he saw Annie—Carl Reese's daughter—staring back at him.

Chapter 11

Longarm pushed the large empty plate away, patted his belly contentedly, and grinned up at Ma Hightower.

"Thank you, Ma. That should last me until Denver City sinks below the sea. Maybe even longer."

"There's plenty of doughnuts. Made them fresh. And coffee."

Sadly, Longarm said, "I've got to ride."

"No need to ride off without visitin' a spell," she retorted stubbornly. "Ain't neighborly."

"No, thanks. But thanks just the same."

"Leave him be, Ma," said Hightower. He aimed a dark stream at the wooden bucket they used as a cuspidor, and missed.

"I'll see you to your horse," said Asa, disengaging himself gently from Anna May.

From the moment they had ridden up two days ago, the willowy blonde had blossomed about Asa like a flower that could never wilt. As silent and as devoted as a shadow, she filled Asa's every need as effortlessly as she breathed. It was almost spooky. For Asa, the results had been spectacular. Already he had a healthy tan, and his cadaverous cheeks were beginning to fill out.

Leaving the cabin, Longarm glanced at the gambler. "You going to forget how to fill an inside straight?"

Asa laughed. "An old pro never forgets, Longarm. You should know that. Anna May is just a welcome break in an otherwise melancholy pattern. How long it will last I do not know. And I will not ask the fates to tell me, either."

"Good idea."

They reached Longarm's black, a mount he now regarded as a posthumous gift from Howard Murphy.

"You sure you won't stay a while longer?" Asa asked. "There's plenty of work needing to be done around here. This ruined barn, for instance."

"No way I can wait any longer," the big lawman said, aware that Asa knew only too well what mean choices awaited Longarm. "You saw that telegram. Billy wants me to explain the slaughter—but not before I bring in the Calico Kid."

Longarm stepped up into his saddle and leaned back. The leather creaked comfortably. Then he reached down and shook Asa's hand. "Been nice riding with you, Asa."

"Likewise, Longarm."

Longarm glanced at the cabin doorway. Hightower, his wife, Anna May, and the rest of the clan were watching. He waved and they waved back. Wheeling his mount, Longarm rode out of the compound and set his horse toward Mills Falls.

When first he had arrived back at the Hightower farm, he had been in no hurry to go after Annie Reese. He knew where to find her, and he had more than a hunch—it was a dull, miserable certainty—that she would be waiting for him. The prospect of bringing in Annie Reese was not a pleasant one for Longarm to contemplate. But Annie could wait. Billy Vail wanted the Calico Kid, and so did Longarm.

To his chagrin, until a few days ago the likelihood that Annie Reese and the Calico Kid could be one and the same had not occurred to him. This possibility still amazed him, and for a while he had circled it like a hungry coyote would an aroused rattler, too fearful of the consequences to move closer, but too damned hungry to pull back.

Returning from Cottonwood the day before yesterday, Asa told him that he had heard talk that a desk clerk in Mills Falls had been blabbing about those two men the Calico Kid had killed, then dragged through Main Street. According to the clerk, both men had been lured to their death by a slim young girl—a blonde. The way he was telling it, the last time the desk clerk—or anyone else, for that matter—had seen either Rivkin or Tillson alive, was when they disappeared upstairs in his hotel to play with that blonde.

The moment Longarm began mulling over the desk clerk's tale, he found himself recalling once again Wes Hardy's cryptic reply when Longarm asked him who the Calico Kid was.

Don't you know...? She was nice...enjoyed her, too.

Well, Longarm was pretty damn sure he knew now. And it made his heart ache. But before he went to get Annie, he wanted to ride to Mills Falls, to be absolutely sure. A part of him was hoping desperately that this mouthy clerk was just blowing off steam to attract attention. But this was, at best, a forlorn hope.

"Room for the night, sir?"

"No," said Longarm, taking out his wallet and opening it to show the desk clerk his shield.

The clerk swallowed nervously, his huge Adam's apple bobbing alarmingly. "Yes, Marshal—what can I do for you?"

"You been blabbin' a mite lately, I hear."

The clerk had a pale face and watery eyes. Running a bony hand through his dull hair, he said, "I guess that's a fact—if you mean what I been saying about that . . . girl who was with Cal and Jim before they was murdered. Is that what you meant, sir?"

Longarm nodded grimly.

"Well, ain't that something! I didn't think anyone was payin' the slightest attention. I told just about everybody, but they wouldn't listen. Said I was only destroying the reputations of two dead men."

"Well, you sure as hell weren't doing their reputations any good, were you?"

"Reckon I wasn't, at that." The clerk looked unhappily at Longarm. "But it's the truth, what I saw, Marshal. Besides, suppose I'm right?"

Longarm's eyes narrowed. "About what?"

"That the Calico Kid is a woman."

"You think so, do you?"

"Yes, I do. It don't matter to me *what* everybody else is saying."

"And what's everybody else saying?"

"The word going around is that Wes Hardy was the Calico Kid. That he was shot down in Cottonwood after he raided one of the juror's farms, and that a marshal found on his dead body the calico bandanna he used."

"I was the one there, sonny. I was the one plucked that bandanna from the pocket of Wes Hardy's deerskin jacket."

"You mean it's true?"

"Tell me about this girl, the one you say lured those two men to their deaths."

At once the clerk's eyes brightened. "She was some looker, she was. She wasn't more'n eighteen or nineteen, I'd say, and she didn't fill out a dress all that much, but she had long blonde hair and eyes that really said hello, if you know what I mean."

"She was thin—boyish, almost?"

"Almost, Marshal. But she was really all girl."

"What else can you tell me?"

"She never checked out, and neither Cal Rivkin nor Jim Tillson came back down those stairs over there."

"How do you explain that?"

"She slipped out the window of her room after she lowered those two men she killed to the alley."

"I'd like to see that room now. Is it being used?"

"No, it isn't.

"Let's go, then."

The clerk grabbed the key and led Longarm swiftly up the stairs, dancing nimbly out of his way as he let Longarm past him into the room. Longarm went to the window and looked down. The window faced the alley and the roof of the back porch was directly under it. What the clerk had surmised was entirely possible.

In that instant, all doubt vanished. Longarm knew the identity of the Calico Kid.

"Thank you," Longarm said to the clerk, as he turned from the window and left the room.

Closing the door hastily after him, the clerk called down the stairs to Longarm, "Marshal! What do you think? Could I be right?"

Without pausing, Longarm called back to the clerk, "Beats the shit out of me, sonny," and left.

Annie had been expecting Longarm to come for her as soon as he learned of the death of Howard Murphy. Joanna would surely tell Longarm—as well as any and all who would listen—that it was Annie Reese who had killed Murphy and fired his ranch. And Joanna's description of Annie Reese would surely enable Longarm to make the connection.

For that reason, when Longarm did not come for her immediately, she began to wonder if Joanna could possibly have lost her life in the fire. The only other explanation she could think of was that Longarm might not have received from Joanna a description of the girl who had shown up at the Lazy M to kill Howard Murphy.

But those doubts were behind her now. Longarm had undoubtedly asked the obvious questions and come up with the right answers. Now, hidden by the pines that crowned the ridge below her ranch, she watched Longarm approach. He was riding across a parkland, heading straight for the ridge. She had expected him to be coming from the direction of Murphy's spread. Instead, he was coming from the west, from the direction of Mills Falls.

She waited until he was close enough for her to see the reins in his hands before she mounted up. Though she did so with considerable care, the exertion caused her to double up, coughing painfully. For a moment the pines swirled drunkenly about her and she had to reach out and grab the saddlehorn in order to stay in the saddle. But the weakness passed. She pulled her mount around and, lifting it to a canter, slanted down the ridge to meet Longarm.

When he saw her coming, he pulled up. She waved. He watched her, but did not wave back.

Oh, damn! she thought bitterly. *How can I go through with this?*

She kept riding toward him and when she drew her Colt, he frowned, but did not go for his own weapon.

"What's that gun for?" He asked her. "That's a hell of a way to greet an old friend."

"If you've come to take me back for the killing of Howard Murphy, I won't go, Longarm. I deserve a medal for what I did to that bastard. He was responsible for the death of my father."

"Yes, that's why I've come, Annie. For that, and for the killings you are responsible for as the Calico Kid."

"So you found out about that too? How?"

"That's not important now, Annie. Put down that gun. It's all over."

"Will I get a fair trail, do you think?"

"Of course."

She laughed. "No, Longarm. I am not going to let you take me in." She raised the Colt. "Turn around now and ride back the way you came. And tell whoever you send to get me that I am not going to go without a fight."

"I am not going to give this job to someone else," Longarm told her. "If anyone takes you in, it'll be me." He smiled thinly. "And if I don't, there's a good likelihood you'll get away scot-free—if you can bear to leave this here ranch of yours, that is."

She considered his words for a moment. "Longarm, please—I told you. I am not going to give myself up—to you, or to anyone else."

"And I told you I am not leaving without you."

167

"You don't believe I'll shoot you."

"Of course I do."

"Then, dammit! Why won't you turn your horse about and leave?"

"You know why. Now put down that gun!"

Her face as cold as her resolve, she aimed point-blank at Longarm and fired. But Longarm had already ducked and, rowelling his horse viciously, he charged Annie. The round whistled past his lowered shoulder as he bolted toward her. Before she could cock and fire again, he had leaped from his saddle and swept her off her horse. Landing in an awkward embrace on the ground, they tumbled a moment, then came to a halt.

Surprisingly, Annie did not struggle or make any effort to pull free of him.

He released her body from his embrace and looked down at her. Her eyes were shut, her face a ghastly gray. For the first time he noticed her sunken eyes and the deep circles under them. He slapped her gently to arouse her, but got no response. From the look of her, she was hurt bad. This surprised Longarm. The high grass had not been that hard to land on, and he had done his best to cushion her body when he came down.

Sticking her Colt into his belt, he slung her slight frame over his shoulder and led both horses beyond the ridge and up the long trail to her place. It took him the best part of an hour. In all that time, Annie did not stir once. But what really alarmed him the most as he trudged along was the growing realization of just how incredibly light his burden had become in the few short days since last he had held her in his arms.

Reaching her cabin, he kicked open the door and let her down on her bed. He went back, closed the door, then, using the hand pump by the sink, filled a basin with water. Dropping a towel into it, he returned to the bedroom. Wringing out the towel a little, he folded it and placed it over her forehead. She still looked very bad, and he was beginning to worry.

He waited patiently. At last, he grew so worried, he leaned his head onto her chest and listened for a heartbeat. He found one, but it was incredibly faint.

When he straightened, her eyes were open and she was staring up at him in wonder.

"I didn't kill you," she whispered, delighted.

"Not because you didn't try," he told her ruefully.

"I love you," she said.

"That's right. Try to kill me, then say you love me."

"That has nothing to do with it. Besides, I needn't have worried. You wouldn't have let me kill you. I'm no match for you. I'm just a slip of a girl."

"Some slip. Some girl."

She tried to smile, but couldn't. "I'm tired, Longarm. Very tired."

"You don't look good. Not good at all. What's wrong, Annie?"

"Open my shirt, Longarm."

He unbuttoned her shirt and opened it. She did not have to tell him what to look for. He saw it at once: a dark, ugly purple patch under her right breast. There was a tiny black hole in the center of it. Looking closer, he saw that her entire chest was slightly distended.

"What in hell is it?" he asked. "An insect bite of some kind?"

"The insect was Joanna Rawlings. She stuck me with a hatpin. It wasn't so bad at first, but I guess she found something vital, sure enough. I can't eat any longer, and I've been coughing up blood for days."

He took the towel off her forehead and placed his

169

hand gently down on it. Despite the cooling effect of the wet cloth, he could feel the heat raging within her frail body.

"You're running a fever," he told her.

"Yes. For some time now."

"I'll get you to a doctor."

"No, you won't You'll let me stay here. You'll let me die up here in the cool hills. There will be no trial. And maybe you'll find a spot for me on that ridge back of the pine hill."

"Dammit, Annie."

"Now there's no need for tears. I'm a killer. Hell is my destination as sure as there's a God in heaven and a devil waiting below. But don't you see? This solves everything. You couldn't kill me, even when I raised a gun to kill you. So how could you have taken me in?"

"I'd have taken you in, Annie."

Her face broke into a dim smile. "All right, lawman. I'll give you that. You would have taken me in if I had let you. Even if I hadn't, I suppose. But we don't have to think about that any more. Joanna has made it all quite simple for us."

"I suppose." He cleared his throat. "Annie, about Pete Bergstrom. Did you really have to kill him?"

"I didn't trust him. I thought he was going to shoot you in the back. He's done worse."

"I don't think he would have."

"You'll never know, Longarm. And neither will I. But it is a judgment on my soul, not yours."

He patted her hand to comfort her, but she looked quickly away. For a while he could think of nothing to say, which was strange, since he had so much he wanted to ask her. Then he looked down and saw her wide, feverish eyes staring up at him with all the forlorn hopelessness of an abandoned child. It reminded him of something.

"You must have loved your father very much, Annie."

"Carl was all I had and I was all he had. I was his bastard daughter, but he spared no expense to see that I got the best schooling and upbringing money could buy. He bought and stocked this horse ranch for me. We planned to run it together when he retired."

"All this must have been expensive."

"I tried to tell him he didn't have to do it, but he wouldn't listen. That was how he got tied in with Murphy. Murphy gave him a cut for every Lazy M head he allowed into the stockyards with a questionable brand."

"But he got too greedy, and Murphy had him killed."

"Yes," she said, her eyes suddenly filling with tears. "You don't know how I pleaded with him to break with Murphy. But all he could think of was this ranch—and what he could buy for me."

Longarm nodded and patted her hand.

"Longarm," she said, her voice soft.

"Yes?"

"I want you to know. I am not sorry about those jurors I killed. Not about any of them. They deserved to die. Just as I do now."

Longarm shuddered slightly. Looking into Annie's fading blue eyes, he realized that there would never be a way for any man—least of all, him—to fathom the soul of this woman.

He cleared his throat and asked, as gently as he could, "Did Wes Hardy discover you up here?"

Her mouth became a hard line. She turned her head so she would not have to look into his eyes. "Yes. After you rode out the last time, he visited me. He was not ... gentle. I'm glad I killed him."

"That was when he took your calico bandanna from you."

"Yes."

He took her hand in his. It was on fire. "How do you feel?"

"If you want the truth," she said wanly, looking back up into his face, "terrible."

"I'll make you a broth. You need something in your stomach—nourishment of some kind."

She managed a smile. "Yes," she said. "That sounds like a good idea."

Longarm had finished rummaging through the root cellar and was busy peeling some potatoes. He had kindled a fire in the stove and the water for the stew was beginning to heat up. All the while he worked, he was miserable with the knowledge that Annie would never sip any of the broth he was preparing for her. But, desperate for something to occupy his mind, he kept himself feverishly busy.

He was reaching for the water on the stove when he heard Annie calling his name. It was like a voice from another world, so faint was it. He slammed down the pan of water and hurried into her bedroom.

A steady stream of blood was issuing from one corner of her mouth. It was the color of India ink. Her eyes were closed and she seemed to have sunk almost out of sight into the bed. She opened her eyes as he sat down beside her.

"Maybe I am a little sorry, Longarm," she told him in a voice he had to strain to hear.

"Don't try to talk," he told her.

"What I mean is, I am sorry we didn't meet un-der...different circumstances."

"I am too," he managed.

She saw the tears rolling down his cheeks and reached up to wipe them away.

"Don't cry for me," she whispered. "Please."

He nodded blindly. Her hand dropped and he leaned forward to brush her hair back off her brow. When he looked back down into her face, he saw that she was gone.

Chapter 12

"But the carnage, Longarm!" Billy cried, shaking his head in disbelief. "The awful carnage!"

Longarm puffed on his cheroot and looked again at the banjo clock on the wall. He knew Billy had to get this off his chest or he would have a major attack of dyspepsia, or whatever the hell it was a man got when he swallowed instead of spitting out.

"Yup," said Longarm agreeably. "It was awful, Billy. Simply awful."

"Cochise!" Billy cried, his voice rising to a quavering wail. "Cochise himself, for Christ's sake, didn't strew the countryside with this number of corpses! Sweet bleeding Jesus, Longarm! All them jurors, Wes Hardy, Howard Murphy—and that Lazy M rider . . ." He looked wildly at Longarm for help. "What was his name?"

"The one that came at me with a knife?"

"Yes, dammit!"

"Red something-or-other."

"My God, Longarm! You don't even know his name."

"Don't you have it right there in your report, Billy?"

"That ain't the point!"

Longarm uncrossed his legs and peered with some concern across the desk at Billy Vail. "Are you aware, Chief, that two members of that jury are still alive and well?"

"Sweet Jesus, Longarm! Is that your measure of success? Two jurors alive, ten dead!"

"Aw, hell, Billy," Longarm drawled, "you know that damn well wasn't much of a jury. And you ain't mentioning that the Calico Kid is no longer a threat to your district."

"What makes you so sure, dammit? You didn't bring the son of a bitch in, that I can see."

Longarm took the cheroot out of his mouth and fixed Billy with a long stare. "He's out of action, Billy."

"You mean he's gone into retirement," Billy snapped with weary exasperation. His engine was beginning to run down. "Is that it?"

Longarm shrugged.

"What truth is there in this rumor that Wes Hardy was the Calico Kid?"

Again Longarm shrugged.

"And that crazy girl, the one who set fire to Murphy's ranch and killed him, the one who said she was Carl Reese's daughter! You sure there's no trace of her? She just vanished?"

Longarm nodded. "Like the ground up and swallowed her."

Billy Vail took a deep breath and ran his pudgy hand

over his face. It appeared to help some. When his beefy countenance emerged, the red splotches on his cheeks had subsided somewhat, and the wild light in his eyes had faded to a miserable gleam.

It was time, Longarm decided. He had had enough.

"Billy," he said, leaning abruptly forward in the red leather chair, "when you called me in here a few weeks ago, you were fit to be tied because a killer name of Wes Hardy had got off scot-free for murdering Carl Reese. Hardy has now gone to see his Maker, along with those who engineered that sweet miscarriage of justice, including the man who paid Wes Hardy to kill that inspector."

Longarm got up.

Billy Vail leaned back in his chair, his outrage of a moment before fading swiftly as he saw that he had angered his best operative—and sure as hell the one he most respected.

Longarm smiled to take some of the edge off his words. "I ain't God. I ain't even very smart. And if a bullet hits me, I bleed. If a pretty gal nudges me, I get ready. I put my pants on one leg at a time. So the next time you want miracles, Chief, call on somebody else."

Plucking his hat off Vail's desk, Longarm clapped it on. "When you calm down, Chief, you know which bars I frequent."

He turned and left Billy's office. With calm, measured anger, he slammed the door.

William Clancy Bergstrom wiped some horse manure off his pitchfork with the heel of his boot and squinted crookedly up at Longarm. "Yup, that's my name, sure enough."

"Your father was Pete Bergstrom?"

Young Bergstrom nodded. "That's Pa, all right. How's

the old son of a bitch doing out there on that damn crag?"

"He's dead, William."

Longarm waited for a reaction. There was none that he could see. William pursed his lips thoughtfully. "Well, he was getting on," his son said. "No one lives forever, not even that cold-hearted bastard."

"I was with him when he died."

"That so?" William seemed totally uninterested. He actually seemed anxious to get back to pitching horse manure.

"His last words were about you. He wanted you to have his place."

William frowned up at Longarm for a moment, comprehension slowly lighting his face. "That's why you came by?"

Longarm nodded.

"Well, if that don't beat hell. The old man giving me something." He shook his head in wonderment.

"His place is yours if you want it," Longarm said. "I'm your witness that he wanted you to have it."

"I been there, mister. You ever been there?"

"I was there."

"Then you know what I mean. He didn't give that place to me because he wanted to please me. He gave that place to me as a punishment. There ain't no way you could get me to live out there."

"You don't want his place, then."

"Goddamn right, I don't."

Longarm stood there lamely, not knowing what else to say. He had not expected this kind of a response. Land was land. There was a house on it, of sorts. And livestock. For some, it would be a hopeful beginning.

"You don't have to feel bad," said William. "I thank you for coming all this way to tell me. But I'm just fine

178

right where I am. Some people have to go a lifetime to find their true calling. I found it early on, right here in this stable—shoveling shit. Good day, sir."

Not long after, feeling only a little better, Longarm emerged from a saloon on Larimer Street. Ignoring the flood of scurrying city folk, he adjusted his hat very carefully, then glanced about him for inspiration as to his next port of call.

"Why, it's Deputy Long!"

Longarm turned to find himself looking into the bright face of Ellen Shoenburg. Her somber countenance had turned to the sun, it appeared. She was a transformed woman, and evidently very glad to see Longarm again.

Longarm, on the other hand, was not so eager to recall the events of these past weeks. There were a few things— and one sad burial in particular, high in the hills above a horse ranch—that he very much wanted to forget.

"Howdy, Miss Ellen," he said solemnly.

"But isn't this a coincidence!"

"No, ma'am, it isn't. I distinctly heard you say you was coming to Denver City to visit your mother's folks. Have you sold the ranch yet?"

"Yes," she said brightly. "To a very enthusiastic gentleman from Scotland. I do believe he plans to make a fortune running cattle."

"You didn't do anything to discourage him, I presume."

"There was no way I could have."

"Sounds like a Scotsman."

She stood before him, smiling up at him. Longarm realized then that it was his move next. "Would you care to join me in a drink?" he asked her, smiling.

She smiled right back at him. "You have just left a

saloon, I noticed. No, it wasn't a drink I was thinking of, Longarm. It was something else."

She was so forthright, she was taking him by surprise. "I don't understand."

"You understand perfectly, Longarm."

"Yes, I suppose I do."

"In Lakewood City you comforted me the way a man should comfort a woman. And you were every inch the gentleman. Now I would like to comfort you. You appear to need some comforting right now."

"You are a shrewd, observant woman, and that's a fact."

"I hope you will have occasion to describe me in other terms when this day is done. Do you have a place, Longarm?"

He extended his arm and tipped his hat. "Yes, I do, Ellen. Allow me."

Longarm was standing by the window, looking down at the dark city, the street lamps flaring dimly, the smell of burning leaves heavy in the night air. He heard the bedsprings squeak behind him as Ellen left the bed and approached him. Her slender arms encircled his naked waist as she rested her chin on his shoulder and gazed past him down at the city.

"What's that smell, Longarm?"

"Like someone burning leaves?"

"Yes."

"Someone burning leaves."

She laughed. "Oh, Longarm!"

He swept her up in his arms and carried her back to the bed. Dropping beside her, he pulled her closer and kissed her on the tip of her nose.

"I am ready to describe you in other terms now, Ellen," he said, nipping at her earlobe. "Passionate, tender, warm . . ."

"Shut up," she sighed. "We'll talk later."

And they did, but it was much, much later.

Watch for

LONGARM AND THE FRENCH ACTRESS

fifty-fifth in the bold
LONGARM series from Jove

Coming in May!

6